FROM THE TOP

A SECOND CHANCE NOVEL

BRITTNI MINER

EBURNEAN
BOOKS

EBURNEAN
BOOKS

FROM THE TOP

For Shenandoah: The road leads back to you

CHAPTER 1

"*I*t's running backwards again, Mom."

Lizzie twisted onto her side, rolling herself up into her papery sheets like a nestled caterpillar. She cracked one eye open a slit to see the time. Through the haze of her darkened bedroom, 6:03 branded itself onto her retina. Awake.

"Fullmer, we've talked about the *Spider-Man* rule," she groaned.

"Joke's on you, Mom, they're playing reruns!" Hazel flew into the room past her twin brother, a mess of tangled, kinky blonde curls that landed with a *poof* on the crumbling mattress. "*Spider-Man* is on all morning starting super early, then *The X-Men*. You know, for that new movie coming out." Hazel clambered up onto the pillow and then eased her way slowly under the patchy quilt. She rolled herself to her side, just as her mother had, dragging with her Lizzie's last vestige of warm, cozy sleep time. "Mmm, feels good in here."

Lizzie snatched back the covers and buried herself until the room was darkness once more. "I can still drop you guys off at the fire station," she griped. "There's no age limit on that. No questions asked." Hazel's giggle was muffled through the quilt, but Lizzie could still picture how her daughter's cheeks were turning rosy pink as she laughed.

"*Mom*, it's running backwards."

Fullmer's voice was impatient, serious. Lizzie pulled back the quilt and sat up. She was the parent, but her son was the adult. Fullmer was short and scrawny, but his dark green eyes begged to be taken seriously. A worried frown tugged down the corners of his mouth. He favored a set of blue and red polos that Lizzie had found at a yard sale a year back and he wore one now, the collar ironed sharp and crisp and making him look like a shrunken down forty-year-old who had come to lecture her about staying out past curfew.

"Mo-om, it's the Coltrane!" Impatient, he stamped his foot. Ah, there was the nine-year-old.

Lizzie smiled and sighed. She reached over to her night-stand and grabbed her last hair tie, which barely hung together by a thin, dying rope of elastic. She held the band between her teeth as she swept up her own tangled mess of blonde curls. "The record player can't 'un 'ackerds—" She twisted the hair into a lopsided bun "—The guy said so."

"It can and it does. I have played it twenty-three times and I'm sure."

"Stop counting, dingleberry." Hazel flicked her brother on his forehead. Lizzie felt the impulse to swat her away but stopped short when she saw the half smile that threatened to overtake Fullmer's face. Thank God for twin camaraderie.

Sometimes it was still hard to believe that these kids were hers. And yet, the evidence of both her parenting and genetics were clear in their every action.

Sometimes this was for the better, like how Lizzie's creative drive lent itself to Fullmer's easy acceptance of his individuality and Hazel's sense of excitement and wonder. Other times, though, seeing her shortcomings in her children made Lizzie cringe. Hazel had developed a boy obsession as of late, and Lizzie couldn't help but think that the infatuations were linked to her desire to have her own family one day, with the picture-perfect husband and the 2.5 kids. It was something Hazel had never had in her own life, and Lizzie couldn't exactly blame her for reaching out for a stability that was just beyond her reach.

Even more troubling was Fullmer's counting preoccupation, a habit which had started out as the occasional annoyance and recently developed into a full-on compulsion. Unlike Hazel's desire for companionship, this new parenting development baffled Lizzie. Was the counting Fullmer's own way of bringing order and predictability into his otherwise uncertain world?

Lizzie tried to keep her addressing of the habit light and without too much chastisement. But still, her heart ached just a little every time she heard him going at it under his breath. It was a painful reminder that despite any extra shifts she picked up at work or parenting books she rented out from the library, there were just some things that her status as a poor, single mother would hinder her from fixing.

She pulled both kids onto her lap. Hazel curled into her, head resting on Lizzie's shoulder like a faithful pup. Fullmer squirmed, wrenching himself free to implore his mother with a more direct stare.

"Twenty-three times!" He pinched the bridge of his nose and Lizzie could practically envision a table of tax documents or consent forms in front of him. "The *Giant Steps* album is a catastrophe. And don't even get me started on the

Village Vanguard stuff. Coltrane's jazz has been murdered."
He pouted, one fat lip sticking out.

"Honestly, Mer, I don't know how you can even tell. It's all a jumbled mess to me."

Thoroughly exasperated with her, Fullmer slid off his mother's lap and headed out toward the living area, his body hunched over with the weight of Lizzie's ignorance. Hazel grinned up at her mother with gapped teeth. "Drama queen," she laughed and shrugged, hopping off to follow her brother.

Lizzie stood up slowly, the world spinning a bit underneath her as she found her footing. When did she get in last night? Two? Kavinsky had been harassing her again, adding on to the closing list while he tried to cajole her into having a nightcap with him. She probably still had greasy black pomade stains on her apron from where he'd been grabbing at her all shift. Skeez.

Just the thought of her ghoulish boss made Lizzie's skin light up with goosebumps. She'd grown accustomed to his treatment; she expected it even. That was life as a woman, she figured. One harassment after the other. But that fact didn't make it any easier to endure. The thought of his fingers brushing her thigh made her feel a wave of dizziness all over again. Best to just ignore those kinds of thoughts. She started toward the family area.

God, the tile was freezing. Their whole apartment was tile. Who did that? Who thought, What a brilliant idea! What could make a dollhouse-sized apartment even more cozy? Tile! Sell 'em like hotcakes, baby. Lizzie cracked her toes before sliding her feet into her sagging pink slippers by the door.

In the living room, the kids had already stacked themselves under a shared quilt. Hazel sat cross-legged on the paisley couch, the remote balanced between her naked toes. Fullmer lay on his tummy, the patchwork draped over his head and shoulders as he fidgeted with his record player on the end table. Garbled saxophone notes buzzed through the air, pushing at a headache Lizzie hadn't realized she had.

"Don't mess with it, baby. Maybe I can have the antique guy take a look if he comes in for lunch today."

Lizzie shivered and grabbed her jacket from off its hook on the wall, pulling it over her pajamas. Heat must be out again. She was so sure she'd paid that one. She rolled up her sleeves before opening up the fridge to pull out the eggs.

"French toast?" she asked the room. Neither kid looked up. She turned back to the kitchenette, just then realizing that she'd used up the end of the bread on breakfast the day before. "Just kidding. Scrambled eggs it is."

Lizzie's cell phone rang, the bright, clear voice of Sutton Foster cutting through the mindless hum of Saturday morning television.

"IT'S A CALL, MOM!"

"*Thank you, Hazel.*" Lizzie smirked and shook her head. She walked over and hip-bumped her daughter's head as she stirred the eggs in the pan.

Hazel turned to her, bright eyes lighting up. "Oh God, Mom, Greta's party!"

"Don't worry, I didn't forget." Lizzie wiped her hand on her sweatpants before fumbling to mute her phone. NORA flashed across the screen insistently.

"I need to change, it's at the roller rink!" Hazel whirled into her and Fullmer's shared bedroom, long streaks of hair barely missing the door that shut behind her.

NORA.

This was the third call in no less than two days. Something twisted in Lizzie's stomach as the thought of Poppy, lifeless and gray on his practice floor, came flooding into her mind's eye. She'd ignored Nora's first two calls, thinking that it was a check-in with bad timing. She had already imagined how the conversation would play out: *Kids doing alright?* Yes, Nora. *Diner ok?* Yes, Nora. *Do you have enough money?* Yes, Nora.

She really shouldn't complain. Outside of Kavinsky, the super, or Mrs. Schmidt from next door, Nora Grant was the only person who bothered to call Lizzie, and she always had the best of intentions. Lizzie could practically feel her warmth carried across the wavelengths, radiating out from the tinny iPhone she had sent her one year for Christmas. She offered support and sometimes checks. Above all, she offered the kind of intense, unquestionable friendship that sticks to the bones.

Lizzie had met Nora in the ninth grade. Her mom had just bailed—for real, this time, not just on one of those benders that brought her back, crying, after a long weekend. Lizzie had come in to the first day of school wearing hand-me-downs from her dad's new live-in girlfriend and smelling like his Coors and bad weed. She had been able to feel the pink stain of her humiliation stamping the back of her neck, branding her with a blazing message: *Don't Get Involved, Guys.*

The other kids didn't look twice at her, but Nora did. She sat down right next to Lizzie (on the roll, Grant came just before Hancock), extended one manicured hand and chirped, "You must be Elizabeth! I saw your name on the desk during the open house. Great eyeliner!"

And that was that. Best friendship formed on alphabetical order and a single observation. Nora opened the door for Lizzie's life to change and, for that, she'd continue to pick up her random phone calls, even if that familiar blush crept back onto her neck whenever she knew she'd have to reveal the intimate details of her private life in Nowhere, New Jersey.

NORA.

Lizzie jumped. She put the phone to her ear.

"Is Poppy okay?"

"Lord! What?" Nora's soft, tinkling laugh broke up the end of her drawling question. "Whatever made you think Poppy wasn't okay?"

Lizzie slumped against her refrigerator in relief. "God, Nor, don't scare me like that. He's getting old, ya know."

"I didn't mean to scare you! And don't tell him he's getting old. You should have seen his face at his retirement party last year. Unadulterated seething." Nora laughed again, immediately putting Lizzie back at ease. She stirred the eggs absentmindedly, enjoying the comforting familiarity of the conversation.

"What can I do ya for?" She asked. "We're alive, the apartment hasn't burned down, and the kids still have all their vital organs."

"Well, praise Jesus for that." Lizzie could hear the humor in her friend's voice but could still picture her touching her heart the way she always had at Sunday School whenever she'd felt relieved. Lizzie took a bite of the egg, testing it out.

"I've actually called to offer you a job here in Georgia."

Lizzie spat the egg across the room, its searing hot butter leaving a bright burn on her lips. "God, did you take up meth since we spoke at Thanksgiving? Does Jove Peterson still deal?"

"Very funny," Nora replied. "You can joke about Jove, but he's actually looking a lot better these days. I just saw him come through the practice last month. He had the Air Force haircut and everything." Lizzie could hear the catch in her friend's breathing as she paused in that funny little way she always did, gearing up to present her well-thought out monologue.

She crossed her arms and peeked around the corner to spy on Fullmer, who still looked lost in the puzzling wonders of his ancient record player. She lowered her voice. "There's no way in hell I'm coming back to Georgia. I really thought that would be apparent by now."

"Look, it doesn't have to be a permanent thing," Nora cleared her throat, likely weighing out which words she'd choose next. "It's just that I'm working at the practice now, Bill has been getting really involved with the church, and Poppy is going to lose his mind if his retirement is spent taking care of the girls instead of fishing at Lake Tobo. We could really use ... a nanny."

"A nanny." Lizzie repeated the words blankly, not even bothering to test out how they felt.

Nora rushed into her explanation. "I know, I know. It's not Broadway. It's not even—"

"Nora, I'm not on Broadway now. I'm waiting at a glorified truck stop in Jersey. I've never—" Lizzie could hear her voice picking up, and she peeked back to make sure Fullmer still wasn't listening. She forced herself to whisper once more. "It's not like I'd be giving something up. That's not the point."

"We've got two extra rooms. Enough money for a decent salary. And health care is on me!" She joked.

"Nora..."

For a moment, the line was quiet.

"It's been a decade, Liz. Not many people get a new chance at their old home."

The doorbell rang.

"It's Greta!" Hazel shrieked, racing from her bedroom

with old roller skates clacking together over her shoulder. "Bye, Mom!"

"Check in with the neighbors when you get back!" Lizzie turned back to the kitchen and busied herself once more, sliding the scrambled eggs onto a clean plate and pulling the orange juice out of the fridge. "I've got to go, Nora. I'll call you soon."

"Wait, maybe you could—"

Lizzie clicked off the phone and slid it across the counter as far as she could. She did her best to ignore the feeling of panic that rose involuntarily in her chest. She hadn't committed to going home to Georgia, and she certainly wouldn't the next time Nora called back. There was no need to feel so stressed so immediately.

And yet, her breathing faltered. Her tongue felt awkward in her mouth and tasted acrid. Amazing how the mere thought of returning to the familiar faces of her childhood could elicit such a physical reaction in Lizzie.

Fullmer came ambling into the kitchen with a record tucked under one arm.

"Took four and a half minutes," he said as he sat down in front of his meager plate of eggs.

"Stop counting, dingleberry," Lizzie muttered as she sat down across from him.

Fullmer shrugged and looked up at her with big, shining blue eyes. "Are you taking me to Greta's party, too?"

Lizzie felt a familiar pang in her stomach. They'd had this conversation a million times before, and it never got any easier. She hated seeing Fullmer feeling left behind, especially when his twin—the one person in the world bound to him from conception to the grave—was so readily accepted by her peers.

"No, bud," she answered. "You're hanging out with Mrs.

Schmidt today. She told me yesterday that she might bake cookies!"

Fullmer rolled his eyes. "She only ever bakes snickerdoodles. Old lady cookies."

"Come on, little dude," Lizzie insisted through a mouthful of egg. "Any cookie tastes good before noon!"

He couldn't help himself—Lizzie saw the smile start to crack through until it overtook his whole, freckled face.

"Now eat your eggs so you can go change," she told him. "I've gotta drop you off after I get ready for my shift."

After a cold shower and several agonizing minutes of forcing Fullmer to change into something that didn't make him look like a middle school principal, they were out the door and down the hall. Mrs. Schmidt was in her doorway as they walked up, inserting her key with one shaky hand as she tied her scarf with the other.

"Oh, Mrs. Schmidt! Did we get our days crossed?"

"Elizabeth!" Mrs. Schmidt dropped her key as she clutched her heart. "I am so sorry! Is my sister. Had another attack. Is at Saint Mary's! I go see her now."

"Yesss." Lizzie elbowed Fullmer in his moment of satisfaction. He stopped his celebration to retrieve the key.

"I'm on shift in half an hour," Lizzie said, stepping closer to Mrs. Schmidt's door. "Can he come with you?"

"Am so sorry, Elizabeth!" The old woman shuffled over to the stairs and began to start her slow, fumbling descent. "Wish I could help."

"What do I do with Fullmer?" she asked, her voice desperate.

"Will see you Monday!" Mrs. Schmidt called up the stairs.

"I—" Lizzie turned back to her son, only to see him

already buttoning up his coat and looking up at her expectantly.

"Do you think Mr. Kavinsky will let me play my jazz at the diner this time?"

Lizzie sighed and rubbed her face with both hands, trying to clear her head at bit. She nodded down at Fullmer and motioned for him to lead the way down the stairs.

She couldn't help it. The thought itched at the back of her mind. A warm, clean home. Help if she needed it. Friends for Hazel. For Fullmer.

But she had come this far. Well, she had come... to New Jersey. And that was something, right? She couldn't go back to Georgia. She wouldn't.

CHAPTER 2

For as long as Lizzie had worked there, the Starshine Diner had been popular for no good reason at all, other than its lucky location across from a local theater. Day shifts would drag by with only a handful of people coming through the grimy, clouded glass doors, but at night—at night!—the place would transform into a massive cast party.

Performers would start straggling in around 9:30, always the types who Lizzie imagined used Pond's Cold Cream to carefully remove the last vestiges of their melting makeup, hang their costumes in an orderly fashion, and then proceed across the street to warn the Starshine crew that a large party would be following soon. Lizzie would have the menus counted out and the coffee warm and intoxicating just in time for a gaggle of performers to come bursting through the doors, laughing at some improvised scene from the last performance or belting out the lyrics to their finale number.

Lizzie could never decide how she felt about their presence at the Starshine. In another lifetime, she had been a performer. Now she hummed along when the actors came in singing, and yet she'd dread going over to wait on their tables. She felt naked standing there, smiling, in her plain pink apron. A voyeur into a life part of her wished that she was still living. She'd swallow down a familiar, hard lump in her throat as they quoted Neil Simon or improvised a song lyric, and wish with desperation that Tina could have just taken these tables and left her with dish duty.

Praise the powers that be, Lizzie was on her way into a lunch shift and the diner—as per usual in the harsh chastising daylight—was empty, dirty, and just the way she preferred it. She ushered Fullmer through the glass doors and tried to sweep him into a corner booth before anyone could take notice.

"I'm not a daycare, Hancock."

Shoot.

Kavinsky was heaving his massive form out from behind a spot at the back counter. Her boss was a permanent staple at the Starshine Diner, but Lizzie fancied that she had become pretty good at avoiding unnecessary contact with him. With his iPad out playing *The Hangover* at a low volume and his old cup of coffee sweating a moist ring onto the counter, it looked like today Kavinsky had set up shop to exercise a little power lording more directly over his dominion.

"Mrs. Schmidt had a family emergency," Lizzie said to him as she squatted to help her son to unbutton his coat.

"Five, six, seven..." Fullmer muttered to himself, counting the buttons as Lizzie finished up. She turned her attention back to Kavinsky, plastering a grin onto her face as he crossed his arms and stood before her, eyeballing her son as though he had brought the plague to the Starshine. On instinct, Lizzie placed herself between her boss and Fullmer.

"No," Kavinsky growled, shaking his head.

Lizzie ignored his rejection, broadened her smile in his direction, and maintained a wide berth between them as she slipped her apron over her head and aimed for the kitchen. "Is Tina on this afternoon?"

Kavinsky crossed his arms and shook his head. "You're alone up front, but I'll be here if you need anything." Lizzie was tying her apron when she felt his hand graze her waist. "Anything," he repeated, his monstrous, pock-marked face contorting into what must have been his version of a wink.

She could feel her face grow red and the words she had practiced over and over again were coming out before she could stop them. "I'd appreciate it if you cut that out in front of my kid, Kavinsky. I could quit. Or sue!"

It took more bravery than she'd like to admit to confront him.

"And find work somewhere else in this town?" He snorted, waving her off to return to his post. "Good luck, Broadway. I hear your skills are in high demand.

Lizzie's boss had crossed the line from demeaning to full-on harassing shortly after her job interview. She already hated the Starshine, and Kavinsky made it extra unbearable. The sad truth was she knew that he was right: she desperately needed the work and this was as good as it got. Lizzie had applied around here and there over the years, but there wasn't much for a single mom without a college degree that didn't require her to work at the drop of a hat or take her clothes off.

Not that Kavinsky wouldn't be asking her to do that, too, soon enough.

She stole a glance over at her son, who had settled into

the booth with his feet tucked up underneath him and a massive book on the history of jazz splayed out on the greasy table. A trio of still half-costumed actors entered the diner, and Lizzie gritted her teeth as they passed by Fullmer to settle in near the register. She could feel Kavinsky's eyes on her back as she walked over to hand them menus.

"Matinee, fellas?" she asked as she slid silverware across the counter.

"*Midsummer Night's Dream,*" one of them explained, grinning ear to ear underneath a pair of battered fairy horns. "We're doing a special middle school field trip this weekend."

Lizzie poured coffee in their mugs, and the sprite lifted his in a toast. "To arts education!" She pulled out a pad to take their orders.

Soon the afternoon was in full swing. Lizzie catered to the occasional regular who popped in for coffee or sandwiches, always with an eye on Fullmer in the corner booth, consumed by the tiny details of his own little world. He was a good kid. Focused, diligent. Maybe that was just a nicer way to say obsessed. Still, she loved to watch him, blonde brow furrowed and freckled nose practically touching the pages of his jazz tome. What a kid. After forty-five minutes, he wiggled his way out of the booth and made his way to Lizzie's counter.

"Can I have change for the juke, Mom?"

Lizzie smiled and fished in the pocket of her apron for spare change. She produced a quarter and gave it to a grinning Fullmer, who eagerly hopped over to the jukebox and carefully flipped his way through the short selection of Sinatra. It wasn't Coltrane, but apparently it hit the spot. Lizzie smiled again as she watched him close his eyes and tap out the beat to his chosen song as it blasted through the small diner.

"Hey loser, turn on some real music!"

A wadded straw wrapper pelted Fullmer on the head. Three teenage boys and their scantily clad girlfriends sat at a table by the entrance. With their legs propped up by their waffles and opened sugar packets littering their booth, they chuckled at the brilliance of their ringleader.

The actors at Lizzie's counter rolled their eyes and muttered to each other about absent parents and the need for weekend programs. She watched as the sprite flushed and lowered his head to remove his horns with discretion. "Idiot kids..."

"Hey 'Mer," Lizzie called and gestured to her son, "Why don't you grab your stuff and come hang out with me at the counter?"

Kavinsky interrupted her, popping his greasy black head out from the kitchen. "Hancock. My office." He gestured for the fry cook to cover her spot by the register.

"Oooh, someone's in trouble!" The teenagers called, flicking sugar packets in Lizzie's direction as she took off her apron and followed Kavinsky through the traffic door.

Kavinsky's office was a cave. Stacks of disorganized bills papered his table, chair, and even his keyboard. Half-emptied plates of pie occupied the more empty corners and, as she sat down on the little stool Kavinsky offered her, she had to lift her feet quickly to avoid a bug of unidentifiable origin.

"I'm sorry about Fullmer," she started. "He'll keep the music quiet and—"

Kavinsky waved her off as he collapsed into his seat, the cushion giving an exasperated *oof* under his bulk. "I need you to pull a double on Sunday."

Lizzie shook her head. "I asked for Sunday off months ago. Hazel's got that awards ceremony, and there's no one to watch Fullmer."

Her boss raised a greasy black eyebrow in her direction. "Do you like working here, Hancock?"

Do bodies enjoy the morgue?

"Of course," she answered through gritted teeth. "But I have two kids. Sundays are Mrs. Schmidt's bridge night, so—"

"You'll be here Sunday. George is out for some surgery bullcrap."

"Mr. Kavinsky—"

He rubbed his eyes with the palms of his hands. Lizzie couldn't help but notice the thick black streaks underneath his fingernails. "Hancock, it is always something with you. You think no one wants this job? People are dying in this economy. I could fill your spot in a moment."

Her cheeks burned. "I'm not sure that's entirely fair."

"Here's a fact," he started. "I have very few options on Sunday evenings. It's you or Belinda and, frankly, I can't watch that cow waddling her way around my dining room for another evening shift. It's not my favorite view."

"Sir," Lizzie focused to steady her breathing. "Work with me here. I come in every day."

"Work with you?" His dark eyes shone. She knew right away that she'd said the wrong thing. Kavinsky's meaty face cracked into a smirk. Lizzie held her breath as he slid his chair closer to her stool. "Maybe you're right, Hancock. Maybe we should work something out."

"I can pull a double on Monday instead. That's usually a better day for me."

"No need for a double on Monday," he leered. "There are other ways to earn your keep around here." He placed his hand on her knee, squeezing it. Lizzie jumped back at the sight of those black nails pressing into her skin. She knocked over a stack of paper and bills balanced behind her stool.

"God, Hancock!"

She scrambled to get to her feet and collect the papers, trying to inch her way past Kavinsky and out of the room as she did so. He stopped her with his hand on the small of her back, pulling her closer. She could smell stale coffee on his hot breath.

"Why don't you stick around after your shift?" He asked her.

"I'm sorry," she muttered, looking down as she pushed her way out of the office. "Those guys out front are going to be wondering where their Cokes are."

The door clanged closed behind her, just missing Kavinsky's wandering hand. Lizzie leaned up against the kitchen wall, steadying herself to go back out front. Kavinsky wasn't going to let up anytime soon; she knew that well. He'd been badgering her for months, and it only got worse when the college kids had gone back to school for the fall and left her as his only bait. She put a hand to her cheek. The skin was hot—she knew it must be bright red. She focused on deep, calming breaths before pushing open the traffic doors. Fullmer was here, and he didn't need to see all that.

Lizzie found her stomach churning again when she entered the front. The teenage boys had surrounded Fullmer at the jukebox, where he clutched the now beaten remains of his jazz history to his thin chest. Sinatra's voice crooned at an obnoxious volume.

"That's real cute, fairy boy," one of the teenagers sneered. Lizzie glanced at the three actors seated at her counter. One of them slipped on his jacket, popping the collar to shield an increasingly pink neck.

"Hey!" she shouted, walking over to the confrontation. She turned the Sinatra off.

"This your mama, baby?" Another boy pushed Fullmer, who tripped backwards and fell into Lizzie. She heard the traffic doors swing open and spotted Kavinsky, his hulking form looming as he watched her next move.

Lizzie brushed off the back of Fullmer's coat and then turned back to the boys. "Your food will be out in a second, guys. Why don't you sit back down?"

The kids laughed and started to amble back to their booth. Lizzie felt a breath release that she hadn't even known she'd been holding. Their acne-dotted ringleader snatched the jazz book out of Fullmer's hands on his way, ripping it the rest of the way until it felt at her son's feet in two jagged parts. His buddies cheered him on from their spots around the booth.

"Cut it out, you little punk!" she hissed at him.

The boy's smirk morphed into a sneer Lizzie felt a knot form in her throat as he walked over to Kavinsky, clearly pointing at her and Fullmer. Her boss handed the teen a notepad, and the kid scribbled something down on it. She could feel her stomach sink as Kavinsky started in her direction.

"Come on, Hancock, harassing my customers? You've gotta get this under control." Kavinsky's voice grated on her ears. He rubbed his forehead, exasperated with her, as he lumbered his way back over to her. "Now I have to give that snot-nosed punk something free so he doesn't send his parents in here. Here's his number, you'll be calling with a to-go dessert for him later tonight."

Lizzie snatched the pad, rubbing her eyes and feeling

utterly miserable. She returned to Fullmer, trying her best to be quick as she checked him over for injuries. "You ok, kid?"

His big green eyes welled up with tears as he clutched the remnants of his book to his chest. She pulled him close, letting him bury his little face in her apron.

"Hancock! Back to work already!" Kavinsky's voice boomed. He shook his head. "God, if you weren't so cute I wouldn't put up with this crap."

Lizzie straightened up. She wasn't blushing pink anymore; in fact, something inside her had just turned icy. She wiped Fullmer's tears. "Collect your things and go wait at the car," she instructed as she straightened her apron, pulled out her pad, and headed over to the table of teenaged boys. She watched as Fullmer did as he was told, exiting the diner with a cling of the overhead bell.

Lizzie marched back to the table of teenagers. "Sir," she started, her voice sugary sweet. She addressed their ring-leader, who turned to her with a cocky, gap-toothed smile. "I know you think my son's cute and that's why you're teasing and flirting with him, but he's just too young for you. You've got to leave him alone."

The teen looked taken aback. His friends elbowed him, laughing. "Whatever, lady." He waved her off and slung an arm over the trashy girl he'd brought in with him. "I have a girlfriend."

"Oh no," Lizzie winced, feigning embarrassment. "I didn't realize you weren't out yet." She leaned in. "I'm so sorry," she whispered. "I should have returned your phone number to you in private."

She held up the notepad and the boys' eyes went wide.

"Dude!" One of his friends laughed. "That's really Jason's number!"

She smacked the notepad down on the table, smiling broadly as she relished in how their own homophobia played out against them. The boy stood up to try to get her to take it back, to admit she was kidding. But Lizzie plowed on to the counter, ignoring the teenage chatter. She had bigger fish to fry.

She popped open the register, which was still thick with bills from the night before. Kavinsky's laziness and disorganization was finally paying off for her; if he was going to forget to clean out the register, then she was going to do it for him. Over sounds of the boy's continued protests, Lizzie grabbed fistfuls of big bills and shoved them into the deep pockets of her dress.

"Hancock! What do you think you're doing?" Kavinsky was booking it over from his booth, his face turning beet red with the exertion. He still had a fresh donut in his hand, clamped between two pieces of parchment paper. He waved it at her in his frustration, sprinkles flying.

"Consider this my severance pay," she told him. She had cleaned out the register and slammed it shut with a satisfying metal clack. "I quit. You're welcome for me not taking more from you in court." She turned on her heel and grabbed her purse, heading to follow Fullmer's path to their car.

"You're not suing me," Kavinsky pronounced. "You can't even quit. You have nowhere to go!"

"I've already got a job lined up," she smirked. She began to open the door but thought better of it. She turned back to Kavinsky, plucking the donut out of his hand. She held her breath: *be brave.* "I'll be taking this, too."

CHAPTER 3

*I*n the end, their apartment looked much the same empty as it did full. Without their furniture, the kids' stuff, the calendar on the wall... Lizzie was beginning to realize that maybe the apartment had always had an empty quality to it. Like she had never really moved in and made a home there at all.

But maybe that was just impossible to overcome when you have such ugly, stark white walls?

She had called Nora back right after leaving the diner. Lizzie had stood barefoot in her kitchen, fingers nervously tapping on the stovetop as she had hammered out the details of a new life in an old, familiar place. Nora had been thrilled, of course, and Fullmer's eyes had gone big and round when he had realized that the day off from work and Mom's rare conversation with another adult meant something terribly exciting: *they were moving.*

Everything happened fast. Lizzie had made the arrangements to leave their building, booked the flight, patted Hazel's back to comfort her when her daughter realized that moving now meant that Aiden Pacheco would never be able to ask her out to the 5th grade Underwater Wonderland dance. The next thing Lizzie had known, they were on an airplane, her twins marveling at the bird's-eye view they were finally experiencing for the first time. They touched down in Atlanta, rented a car, and were on their way.

"Are we there yet?" It hadn't taken long for the cliché to be said. It was their first major trip and Hazel already had her head popped between the driver and passenger seats to bug her mother.

"This is Macon," Lizzie explained. "We're maybe thirty minutes out."

"How can you even tell?" Hazel asked, falling back into her row to go and press her face up against the window. "All the trees look the same."

They didn't look the same to Lizzie. They had started off in their Honda and she had immediately felt the world as she knew it shifting beneath her. Everything was different in Georgia, swiftly fading from the comforts of big city Atlanta into the rich, full forests of her childhood. With each mile they drove, she could feel her stomach clenching tighter and tighter.

They had left New Jersey so fast, Lizzie hardly had the time to feel the panic creeping in. It wasn't until she got well beyond the airport that she started to remember why she'd resisted Nora's call so vehemently. Her fingers were numb as she drove, and she had to shake them out periodically and hold them in front of the AC. Her vision was swimming, so she blasted the 80s rock over the radio. With each passing minute, it was getting more and more difficult to ignore her fears of revisiting her old life.

"Drive faster, Mom!" Hazel hollered. She nestled herself onto her sleeping brother's shoulder.

The car was beginning to pass familiar landmarks.

"Hazel," Lizzie called over her shoulder. "Look, there's the turnoff for Lane's!" Spotting a familiar site—one with pleasant memories, rather than any tied to high school or other childhood embarrassments—felt like a good distraction.

Hazel pressed her face to the glass once more to see Lane Southern Orchard, a staple of Lizzie's bedtime stories. The place had been described to the kids a thousand times, the setting of many of their mother's teenage adventures. "Are we going to pick peaches, mom?"

Lizzie laughed. "It's not quite the right time of year for that," she explained. "But I promise we'll get to it."

In what felt like a breath, they were suddenly there. The forests and cotton fields dissolved and up sprang Warner Robins, Georgia. The geographical heart of the state.

For as long as Lizzie could remember, Warner Robins was a city struggling between two identities, the first of which she drove through as she entered the town. The outskirts of a bustling Air Force base rose up before her. The buildings were old, sturdy, practical. A long line of cars wrapped through the street, waiting for clearance to enter the compound. Lizzie strained her neck to see, just glimpsing men and women in uniform in the distance, laughing at some unheard joke.

Here, the world was completely boxed into order. Everything on Robins Air Force Base had a purpose, with each ticking part moving seamlessly in and out of place as the world pulsed around it. Lizzie thought to herself that the ads TV stations ran on the 4th of July had it exactly right here: middle Georgia was all apple pies, American flags, and citizens boasting NRA stickers on the backs of their massive SUVs.

Both kids scrambled over each other to watch the base

as it faded away, giving way to Warner Robins' most iconic landmark: the carefully trimmed E.D.I.M.G.I.A.F.A.D. hedges. Every child grew up with the acronym plastered onto school t-shirts or binders, never quite knowing if the acronym stood for "Every Day in Middle Georgia is Air Force Appreciation Day" or "Armed Forces Appreciation Day." It changed back and forth, depending on how patriotic the current mayor was. But whatever it stood for, E.D.I.M.G.I.A.F.A.D. had become the unofficial town slogan and a word in its own right, pronounced as five solid syllables. It was a stamp of pure Americana, something for the teens to holler from the back of their pickup trucks on the night of a big football game or beauty pageant contestants to mention with plastic smiles during TV interviews.

"Look," Lizzie pointed out of her window. "That's where I went to high school."

The kids oohed and aahed appropriately as the industrial landscape of the air force base gave way to a dilapidated school campus. Even when Lizzie had gone to school there, Warner Robins High had never been state-of-the-art, and now it looked even more tired and worn out than it had just the decade prior.

Lizzie felt her fingers tingle all over again as the numbness began to return. Could she even picture herself at WRHS? It felt impossible, like it was another girl who had attended there.

"Will we go to school there, Mom?" Fullmer piped up from the backseat, looking genuinely curious.

"Heaven forbid," Lizzie laughed. "With any luck, they'll have this place condemned by the time you guys get even close to attending."

"Were you popular, Mom?" Hazel poked her head back

through the front seats. "Aunt Nora says you were prom Queen."

"I was on prom Court," Lizzie corrected. "Not nearly as cool. There were a lot of us. We had the dance and ceremony out there at the very end of my senior year." She pointed at the football stadium as they drove by. McConnell-Talbert Stadium was large and imposing, the only part of the school that had received any real renovations in the decade since Lizzie was gone. She could still imagine it as it was when she attended there, flooded with students wearing cardinal and white.

Everything that Lizzie had experienced at WRHS was categorized, clean and neat. But this trip was shaking off the dust it had collected at the back of her brain. Passing by the stadium, a lightning bolt of memory flashed across her eyes, illuminating an almost forgotten prom night. Lizzie shook her head to clear it.

Nora hadn't exactly been lying to Hazel. Lizzie had been decently popular. Or at least, she had enough friends at school that she had been extra-dreading the inevitable trip into town that living with Nora would necessitate. She would definitely run into someone, and then she'd be forced to pick up the same old routine she always had as an introvert desperately faking extroversion. She'd wear the same forced smile, repeat the same trite phrases she had used for four years. This time, though, she'd be compelled to field the question she'd been avoiding for ten years: *So what did you get up to after high school??*

Her thoughts were interrupted by Hazel's gasps from the back seat. "God, Mom, it's like we're in a movie!"

"Beverly Hillbillies before the Beverly." Fullmer agreed. He had his face pressed into the glass right next to his sister's.

As if the high school represented some kind of unofficial border, the clean order of the air force base disappeared and the other half of the city—the Warner Robins of Lizzie's youth—rose up around them.

The town had plenty of stoplights and all the major modern conveniences, but there was still something about it that harkened back to the idyllic southern life of old. Mom and Pop shops leaned, their facades beaten by years of relentless country storms, next to freshly painted Chick-Fil-As and Krogers. Groups of men and boys fully decorated in hunting gear weighed down the beds of ancient pickup trucks, while teenagers in flashy new cars cruised the streets next to the Hancocks. Well-worn white steeples adorned every corner, welcoming crowds of rednecks and moderns alike, even though it was a Tuesday night with no traditional service.

And over everything—nothing spared—was the climbing green kudzu. Lizzie had almost forgotten about it after her years spent up north, but now it insisted upon itself, begging to be seen. It was an invasive species; she remembered learning that in elementary school. Thick, leafy kudzu had been brought to America in the 30s as a garden oddity and made its home in middle Georgia, eating its way through every landmark, natural and manmade alike. It knotted and curled, twisted and slithered, a snake that had been settling in and making its home for so long that the locals had accepted it as something as natural as the iconic red Georgia clay.

Even the neighborhoods Lizzie passed were clearly country fusion territory, complete with their own odd mixture of classic Southern homes and crumbling trailer parks. The houses may have been different, but there was a unifying theme that became apparent as the Hancocks drove on. Everywhere, families sat on their front porches, welcoming the sunset from deck swings, comfortable patio furniture, and even the occasional patterned couch.

Dinner was out. Even from her car, Lizzie could spy big, creamy bowls of chicken and dumplings and pitchers of fresh lemonade. Her stomach rumbled in response to the country ritual she remembered from a million witnesses of her youth. It was almost enough to make her happy to be home.

"Can we stop and get food?" Fullmer pressed, answering her unspoken thought.

"Not this time, bucko," Lizzie replied, signaling for a turn into a familiar neighborhood. "Nora is waiting for us."

"Do you think that Mary-Kate will remember me, Mom?" Hazel unbuckled and squeezed through the divider to hop into the passenger seat.

"Whoa, living on the edge there, babe." Lizzie cocked an eyebrow at her daughter, who promptly ignored her to pull down the mirror and check her hair.

"It's been a while," Hazel continued, pulling out Lizzie's purse to fumble for lip gloss. "I hope she still thinks I'm cool."

Lizzie sent up a silent prayer that her daughter's need to please might fade with a little exposure to stability and family life. Maybe the boy craze would let up, too.

"Everyone thinks you're cool," Lizzie said, reaching over to muss her daughter's hair.

"Mo-om!" Hazel complained.

There were no trailers in this neighborhood. Creekside Estates was old and stately, with each home sporting a perfectly manicured lawn with the University of Georgia and American flags waving in tandem at the front doors. Families in this part of town had lived there for decades, with generations simply swapping bedrooms in their ancestral homes as time went by. Towering pines came together to shield the Estates from the rest of the world, making this secluded spot feel like its own little planet within the city. Here were the Haves of Warner Robins.

As she drove toward Nora's home—the one that she, like the rest of the Estates, had inherited from her parents—Lizzie intuited every turn. She recognized mailboxes and well-behaved German Shepherds peeking over white picket fences. It only took a minute for the Grant home to rise up before her, with a familiar presence waving like a madwoman from the front porch.

"Elizabeth Hancock, get over here!" Nora was at their car in a moment, flinging open the driver's door as Lizzie put the Honda in park.

Lizzie felt her face melt into a smile as her friend pulled her in close. "My god, how do you look exactly the same?"

Nora held Lizzie out to take her in, as her childhood best friend did the same thing. Nora Grant was a force, simultaneously sticking out in the deep South and looking like she owned every acre. Her thick, dark hair was swept back into a practical knot at the top of her head, leaving just a few frizzing strands to frame her studying chocolate face. She was impossibly tall and statuesque, and her frame combined with a thin web of fine wrinkles around her smile and brows made her look far older than Lizzie. She could see now how Nora had gained so much respect so fast in the community as a young doctor fresh out of med school; she took after Poppy in her commanding presence.

Lizzie wondered what her friend must think of her. They were both two children deep, but Lizzie had filled out around the hips a bit. Her skin wasn't as taut and creamy. Gray strands were beginning to infiltrate her once bottle-free blonde hair. She shifted on her feet, a quick stab of worry needling at the back of her mind.

"Watch out, Warner Robins, Elizabeth Hancock is making a killer late debut." Nora flashed a dazzling grin at her, instantly easing the pinch. "My Lanta, you can't be Fullmer and Hazel!"

The kids were falling out of the car in their excitement, scrambling to grab their day bags from the trunk.

"Aunt Nora!" Hazel screamed, heaving bags, snacks, and headphones at Nora all at once to tackle her in a hug around the waist. Nora scooped her up, clutching her tight as though they hadn't been apart a day.

"Mary-Kate and Caroline are going to die when they see you! They've got some friends upstairs that have been waiting all day to meet you."

Hazel shrieked and jumped down, rocketing toward the house and not looking back.

"Is that Fullmer hiding back there?" Nora smiled and stepped around to the back of the car where Fullmer was wrestling with his record player. He had begged Lizzie to let him take it as his carry-on, fretting that a bag handler would destroy it if he dared check it.

"I'm not hiding." Fullmer blushed, but hugged Nora just as tightly as his sister had. "Hey Aunt Nora."

"We've got the best place for this," Nora said, helping him lift out his record player. "Bill is always complaining that we need a little more culture in this house and—"

"And Nora's Poppy has the best Coltrane collection," came a deep voice from behind.

Lizzie whipped around, grinning. Poppy stood in the driveway behind her, leaning onto the gnarled wooden cane that he had carved himself years before. Nora's father had aged quite a bit over the decade she had been gone. His hair was electric white, standing out in stark opposition to his deep, smooth skin, and his back had a hunch to it that she didn't remember being there before. Still, he wore the same funny little half-smile that she could recall from a million nights of getting caught after sneaking into Nora's home after curfew.

"Elizabeth," his booming voice called to her. "Welcome home."

"You listen to jazz?" Fullmer couldn't contain his pleasure. Lizzie felt her heart skip a beat.

Behind him, a heavy bag fell to the ground as Nora collapsed into a sneezing fit. "Let me get that, baby," Poppy volunteered, handing his cane off to Fullmer as he stepped forward to retrieve the bag and put a hand on his daughter's back. "What kind of gentlemen doesn't take in the bags?"

"Welcome back to the South, Lizzie," Nora laughed, shaking her head to clear it. "You traded in snow for pollen."

"Ah, how I've missed the winter yellow-land," Lizzie joked. Nora took her hand, and they followed the boys over to the house.

Being this close to the home made Lizzie feel like she was in a strange dream. Every detail was unchanged, carved perfectly as though lifted straight from a page in her memory. When she'd been growing up, it was Poppy and Ma's house, a haven for Nora to take her ragtag group of misfit friends and show them what it was like to have somewhere that they really belonged. Ma had died years ago and the old house was Nora and Bill's now, but it still had that inviting look to it. Lizzie could smell dinner wafting out from behind the screen door and could hear her daughter in a fit of a laughter as she made instant new best friends. The windows had a soft glow and Lizzie could almost see herself and a young Nora, curled up in that top left attic corner, watching the street below as they laid out big plans.

The pair walked up to the porch together and Nora put an arm around Lizzie, squeezing her tight. "What's mine is yours," she said, smiling. "Except Bill, but you don't want him, anyway. He's taken to snoring lately."

And, just like that, Lizzie found herself stepping back into the past.

CHAPTER 4

*L*izzie awoke to the happy sounds of giggles. She squeezed her eyes shut and buried her head in the soft pillow.

"If I get out of bed now, I better not be stepping into something," she said. The giggles got louder. Lizzie turned and opened her eyes. Hazel was peeking over the edge of her bed, along with eight-year-old Mary-Kate, who was a miniature version of her mother, and seven-year-old Caroline, whose dark freckles and tight curls pegged her as Bill Thornton's daughter.

"Dag nab it!" Mary-Kate cursed, and the other girls erupted into more giggles.

Hazel got up and retrieved a bowl of water from the nightstand. "Mary-Kate said that if you put a sleeping person's hand in water, they'll pee the bed."

"Mary-Kate is right," Lizzie said, sitting up and running her fingers through her tangled hair. "We must have tried that on her Uncle Patrick about a thousand times. Never gets old." She winked and the girls laughed again, tearing off into the hallway, presumably to find their next sleeping victim.

Mary-Kate must be a prankster like her father had been. She had the look of her mother, but the spirit of a football player with something to prove to the rest of the team. Lizzie suspected that the pranks would continue for as long as Mary-Kate had something to prove to the slightly older Hazel. No hands would be safe from warm water bowls for a while.

She swung her legs out of bed, taking in the bedroom in daytime. The room was already brilliant with natural light. Lizzie had fallen asleep still in her travel clothes, not even bothering to make her way under the warm patchwork quilt Nora had provided. The two had stayed up late, drinking wine in Nora's childhood bedroom (now Lizzie's room) and talking about the girls, and the twins, and the state of life since Lizzie had left for the Northeast. They'd only gone to bed when Nora had realized she had to get to sleep if she ever hoped to make it into the practice on time for work.

Now, Lizzie could feel that 2 a.m. wine pressing into the back of her skull. She heaved herself up onto the hardwood, fumbling her way over to the dresser and shifting through stacks of Nora's old t-shirts until she found the soft choir shirt she loved to steal back in high school. She peeled her own blouse off and replaced it, then tied her hair into a loose bun and made her way out the door and down the stairs.

"Hancock!" Bill was at the stove, flipping bacon, when he spotted Lizzie. She smiled and waved, trying to steady herself on the stair railing. He set down his spatula and swept her into a bear hug. "I was so sorry to miss your arrival! We're opening up a new church in Perry, did Nor tell you that? I'm so sick of the late nights, but Reverend is trying to get it running by next month."

Somehow the past decade had been even kinder to Bill Thornton than it had been to his wife. Just two years older than her at thirty, he still looked boyish and handsome, eager to make every room he entered a little bit brighter. His soft brown curls were still full and heavy with the lightest touch of gray to them, and he had happy creases around his eyes that gave him a warm, knowing look that he hadn't possessed back in high school. Nora had told Lizzie the night before that Bill worked as a youth pastor with the big church a few miles away. It was easy to picture him in such a coveted community position, leading children and teens with a laugh and smile.

Despite the genteel career path, though, Lizzie could tell that he was still ever the jock; his white undershirt framed carefully manicured muscles and a tight chest. Sweet, accomplished, *and* handsome? And who said that the football players reached their glory days during senior year?

Lizzie playfully elbowed him away and Bill feigned massive belly injury the way he always had during their schtick back in high school. "Hey, Thornton. Thanks for having us."

"It's our pleasure, ma'am. Want some bacon?"

Her stomach rumbled in response. "Read my mind. I'm nursing this headache ever since we drank—"

A cough came from the breakfast nook, drawing Lizzie's attention to Fullmer and Poppy, who were both fully dressed and tinkering with the record player. Poppy's back was straight and stiff, his attention fully focused on the nine-year-old, but that familiar smile pulling at the corner of his mouth gave him away.

"—Since we drank all that water last night!" Lizzie corrected, grinning. "Geez, I forgot how hot Georgia is!"

"We like it that way," Poppy said. "Keeps them Yankees at bay. Where did you say you came to us from again, Elizabeth?"

Lizzie grabbed a washrag from off the counter and chucked it at his head. She laughed and nabbed a piece of Bill's bacon before settling in next to her son in the breakfast nook.

"Poppy says it's playing backwards, too, Mom." Fullmer was earnest as ever, a little sprout of blonde hair poking up at the back of his head like alfalfa.

"It's the darndest thing," the old man said, bracing himself against the table to heave himself up. "I've got a man in town I can take it to. You remember Bobby Stringham?"

Lizzie scarfed down her last bite of bacon and put her hand on Poppy's arm. "What are you doing?" She implored. "I'm the new nanny, remember? I've got all school, extracurricular, and record player duties from now on. Your job is to catch catfish for dinner. I haven't had nuggets in ages."

Bill stepped in, setting a pan of scrambled eggs on the table between them. "C'mon, Liz, no one expects you to start right away. We just want you to hang out with Nora, take some time to—"

"No," Lizzie shifted uncomfortably, eyeballing her son. "I have a job to do. I'm going to do it!" She snatched another piece of bacon off the counter and shoved it into her mouth before bolting for the kitchen door. "Just 'et me get a quick 'ower and I'll 'ave the kids off to school and into 'outine in no time!"

Mouth still full, she made her way back up the stairs and into the bathroom to clean up. After her first hot, steamy shower in months, she padded her way out of the tub and stood in front of the clouded mirror. Hesitant for a moment, she finally let her towel drop.

She'd been in this bathroom a million times. God, she'd stayed with Nora and the Grants so often that she literally had her own key in high school. But the girl staring back at her now was a stranger to the girl who grew up in Warner Robins. Lizzie thought once more of Nora and Bill, looking clean and put together and *adult*. She always liked her hips and thighs, even when they filled out after having the kids. Now, though, they made her blush as she saw them and thought of how they were a far cry from the Broadway-bound dancer girl who used to stand in the mirror and think about her hair or her minor acne. She was still just a kid playing pretend.

Lizzie swallowed down the feelings. She used her towel to dry out her hair, rubbed a little concealer under her eyes, and hoped for the best. Dressing in the same t-shirt and jeans she'd worn from the night before, she headed back down the stairs. Soon, she was back in the Honda, record player and directions from Poppy in her lap, ready to head out.

It surprised Lizzie how easy it was to remember her way around town. She made it to Bobby Stringham's no problem, an aging little shack near the air force base where the old man tinkered with the machine until it churned out more nonsensical tunes that Lizzie couldn't comprehend. After, she cruised the streets heading to Kroger, grocery list in her bag.

Every kid grows up thinking that there is nothing to do in their hometown, but in Warner Robins, they were right. As Lizzie pulled into the bustling grocery store lot, she spotted a cluster of pickup trucks packed in with teens who were vaping and listening to country music. The Kroger wasn't anything fancy, but it was the closest thing her home-town had to a club and, for that, it was always busy. Lizzie found a spot for the Honda near the back of the lot and she headed into the store with her head down.

Sweet tea. Green peanuts. Black-eyed peas. The list, scrawled in Nora's impeccable, curly handwriting, was filled with the flavors of home. Lizzie's mouth watered. That's what she got for shopping hungry. She wondered if Bill cooked breakfast every morning and if she could talk him into grits tomorrow...

One by one, she collected the items she needed and then headed up front to the cash registers. Just as she suspected, the lines weren't packed with people, and yet they were moving at a painful pace as each customer took the time to lay out their life story for the cashier. In Lizzie's line, an older woman with a blonde bouffant and a small dog in her purse bemoaned the vaping teenagers outside. The cashier looked familiar, a brunette who was nodding enthusiasti-cally and adding "Yes'm" at all the right points of the old woman's story. Lizzie waited with waning patience, shifting from one foot to the other as she wondered if Tom's Thunder Salt and Vinegar Chips were still sold in the South and if the Kroger might carry any near the registers.

"Lizzie Hancock?" The old woman was gone, and the brunette cashier had turned her attentions to her next customer. Her bright eyes shown as she waved. "It's Grace Barker! From high school!" She ran around the register, her pair of mint green flip-flops clapping on the linoleum, and scooped a dizzied Lizzie into a tight hug. A rush of memory came back to Lizzie and Grace Barker materialized into the bubbly, popular teen she'd been back in high school. She was older now, but she still had the perfect dye job. Seemed like she still had the penchant for conversation, too.

Lizzie's face was frozen into a smile, her automatic defense mechanism when confronted by a situation beyond her control. Inside, though, the panic had returned. An invisible vice gripped her chest, and each breath became a concentrated, focused effort. She thought briefly of leaving the groceries and bolting for the sliding doors.

"What are you doin' in town?" Grace asked her. She held her at an arm's length, examining her every inch from ratted old choir t-shirt to faded Keds. The mirror from Nora's bathroom flashed through Lizzie's mind.

"Grace! You look fantastic! You work here?" Lizzie tried her best to deflect the question of what she was doing in Warner Robins. Her voice sounded unnaturally cheery and easy-going. Was she even sure that this was really her talking? Her fast-paced breathing was beginning to subside as the conversation took shape, but it still felt to Lizzie a little bit like she was a woman possessed.

Grace's face flushed a bright pink. "Oh Lord, no, I don't work here." She waved her off. "I stay home with little Alex. Boyd just has me filling in. He runs this Kroger. Isn't that somethin'? Who would have imagined Boyd Stewart doin' anything more than throwin' a football? Lord, you did know we was married didn't you? Five years this spring!"

"No." Lizzie smiled and shook her head, feeling a little dizzy from her old classmate's overwhelming welcome.

Another customer got in line behind her, and Grace shooed them away with one hand. "Go to Greg's line, he needs to stop textin' anyway!" Grace turned her full attention back to Lizzie, propping herself up against the conveyor belt and pulling a pack of gum off of one of the racks. She unwrapped a bright pink piece, placing it on her tongue and beginning to chomp enthusiastically as she examined Lizzie once more. "Lord, it's been a decade if it's been a day. Where are you stayin'? How long are you here fer?"

Lizzie cleared her throat. "Um, indefinitely? I'm living with Nora Grant."

Grace's eyes went wide. "Mm, over in the Estates? Lord, you do have nice accommodations. Boyd and I are out in Shenandoah. It's nice, but it's not what it was back in high school. We just put a pool in. Tryin' to up the value, you know."

"And you have a son? Alex, you said?"

Grace put a pink manicured hand over her heart. "Baby Boyd all over again! Mommy's little boy. Are you on Instagram? I've got pictures."

"No," Lizzie shook her head. "I'm not on ... well, I'm not on anything, really."

"Now why doesn't that surprise me?" Grace put a hand on her hip. "You always were a myst'ry, Lizzie Hancock. Whatchu been up to? Broadway? Boyd and I just saw Hamilton at the Fox last year. We try to stay cultured."

"Not exactly," Lizzie said. She fumbled for the right explanation, but another customer got in line behind her just in time to be her salvation.

"*Greg!*" Grace hollered over to the next register and waved the customer off. "You got kids, Lizzie? You look skinny as you was in high school."

"Thank you," Lizzie laughed. "I've got twins."

Grace smacked her gum, visibly excited. "Are they near three or four? Alex always loves a play date."

"Nearly ten, actually."

Grace's eyes went wide once more. Lizzie's stomach turned into an instant block of ice; she knew that Grace was doing the mental math. "Lord, you have been busy... no mister?"

"No mister," Lizzie shook her head, eyes trained on the floor.

"Well, we'll have to remedy that." Grace winked at her. "Surely you've been over to The Red Dirt?"

"That place is still open?" Lizzie laughed out loud, remembering senior year nights spent sneaking over to the only bar and club within several miles.

"Michael White runs it now. 'Member him?"

"Vaguely. But everyone besides our drama club members are basically a blur to me."

"Oh Lord, drama club!" Grace's face lit up, and she did an excited little dance in the aisle. "We need to get you over to the theater! I was just gonna go prep for auditions after this shift. I might be old, but I still like to belt a tune now and again. We're doin' *Fiddler on the Roof*. You can come see the old gang!"

Lizzie's cheeks were burning. She rubbed the back of her neck. A good excuse wasn't coming fast enough. "The Baron Theater?"

Grace pushed her shoulder. "You will *love* it, hon. It's gettin' all these nice renovations, and it's really grown over the last few years. Ashley Walker will be there, and Clint Stone. Did you know he's gay? Got a partner from 'Lanta and everythin'. Real nice guy. And there's Steph and Jessica and—" Her eyes lit up. "Oh Lord, there's David Flannery! You two must have kept in touch, though. You were so close."

"No—"

Grace ran around back to her register, bending down to retrieve a Kate Spade from underneath. She flipped off her light and waved over to Greg, the teenage cashier, whose line was now wrapping around toward the next aisle. "Come with me, I'll give you a ride to my house and we can prep together! You can sing somethin' from high school. I still got a whole booka songs."

"I don't know," Lizzie demurred quickly. *Breathe.* "It's been a long time. I don't even sing in the shower now." She gestured toward her groceries and awkwardly gave a little laugh. "Besides, you never even rang me up."

"The fixins are on me and Boyd." Grace winked. She threw the items into her cart, pulled it out of the aisle, and gestured for Lizzie to follow. "All this stuff will keep in the car just fine. No excuse now, Lizzie Hancock. I talk too fast for you to get a word in edge-wise, anyway."

Lizzie laughed and followed Grace toward the exit, too much of a coward to make up an excuse and too polite to say no. Her old classmate wasn't wrong.

CHAPTER 5

As mischievous, bored teenagers in Warner Robins, Lizzie and Nora had had a light system. On the rare occasions that Lizzie would brave having Nora over to her meager trailer, she'd leave the Christmas lights off to signal that Dad wasn't home. The red and green strands were left up year round, strung around the home in a haphazard manner that signaled their caretaker didn't have much actual care left in him. By the time he'd come straggling home from his favorite bar out in Cochran, Lizzie's dad, Preston Hancock, was always too drunk to notice their twinkling lights outside of the trailer's one dirty window.

Christmas lights on, don't bother coming in. Christmas lights off, beer (and sometimes a little of Preston's stashed weed) was theirs for the taking before the girls ditched the trailer and headed for greener pastures.

The light system at the Grant house got much more use. Poppy and Ma had always welcomed Lizzie, but that didn't change the fact that sometimes Warner Robins teenagers just needed to stir up some mischief.

The back deck light was standard there. If it was on,

Lizzie was free to walk in the door as she pleased, settle down on the couch, and make herself at home whether the Grants were there or not. She loved seeing the back deck light glowing.

If the guest bedroom light was on, that meant Bill was over. Nora and Bill had been going steady since the dawn of time. The two-year age gap and his own status as a high school football god hadn't made a difference to him; he'd wanted Nora Grant, and he'd pursued her relentlessly until the two were inseparable. The guest bedroom had played host to a thousand rites of passage, and Lizzie knew to keep her distance when the light was on.

Then there were Nora's car lights. Those were trickier. Poppy and Ma were the responsible type, always trying to keep their kids on regular hours. Nora would sneak down to her truck and flip the lights after they went to bed. If they were on and Lizzie was cruising the streets with some friend or boy of the week, she knew that she could let herself into the truck to flip the lights back off, climb the lattice at the back of the house, and go hang in Nora's bedroom.

As Lizzie returned from Grace Barker's house, bulging plastic bags of groceries strapped around her wrists, the back deck light glowed. It was probably standard with Bill in the home. Maybe he grilled back there, or maybe the girls were out back scouting for bugs. Still, Lizzie's heart skipped a beat. She made her way down the driveway and let herself in through the garage door.

"Lizzie, you made it!" Nora called to her from the family dinner table, which was stacked high with southern comforts. "After you called, I worried I wouldn't catch you until late again. I know how Grace Barker can talk."

"I think I can recount every detail of the years I've been living away from her," Lizzie laughed. "Did you know that she studied interior decorating at UGA? Her son's middle name is Douglas? Boyd is—"

"*This close* to landing Kroger Corporate," Bill and Nora completed in unison. They laughed and Bill reached over to squeeze his wife's hand.

"Lizzie, can you get the sweet tea going? I haven't gotten to it yet." Nora stood.

"Silly, you just made a pitcher." Bill kissed her cheek and walked to the fridge to produce the drink. He cleared his throat. "All this showing off cooking must be overwhelming you."

Nora smiled and blushed. "We're just getting started. Come have a seat." Nora pulled out the chair next to Poppy, and Lizzie set her goods on the kitchen counter before heading over.

"Mom, Nora cooked and she didn't use the microwave *once*." Hazel's eyes were wide with wonder.

"Isn't that cool? Did you even know that dinner could be eaten at a table instead of in front of a TV?" Lizzie winked at her daughter and leaned across the table to grab a roll. Poppy slapped her hand away.

"Miss Elizabeth, did you leave your manners in New Jersey? In the Grant house we still say grace and do a sharing round before digging in." Poppy elbowed her and winked. He clasped his hands together and closed his eyes with the rest of the family following suit. Lizzie couldn't help but stifle a laugh as she spotted Hazel and Fullmer on the other side of the table, still wide-eyed and baffled. She coughed and showed them how to clasp their hands like the Grant-Thorntons had.

"Dear Lord Jesus," Poppy began. He was using his doctor voice, firm and authoritative. It filled the dining room. "Please bless this food before us today. We are so grateful to have it. We're also grateful that the Hancock family is livin' with us for a while. We pray that they will make this their own home."

A small noise came from down the table and Lizzie peeked open an eye in time to see Nora clasping Bill's hand to her heart in sentimentality. Poppy continued, his voice low and rumbling. "We pray that Bill's project over at the church will continue as planned. We pray that Nora will be able to *cut back her hours*." (This time Lizzie watched as Nora held back a laugh at Poppy's not-so-subtle chastisement). "And we pray that, if it be in thy will, the Jensons next door will finally cut down that overgrown tree in their yard. It's attracting bugs, and I'm tired of gettin' bit. Amen."

The family *Amen*-ed together. "Alright, Hazel, grab a roll and share something about your day." Nora instructed. "Guests go first."

Lizzie's daughter was already bursting with excitement. She snatched a roll from off the top of pile and bit into it, mouth still full while she launched into her description. "Poppy took us by the school to get registered, and they gave me a t-shirt! It's got stuff on it!" She stood up, chest out, displaying a bright red E.D.I.M.G.I.A.F.A.D. shirt with pride.

Lizzie's heart skipped a beat. It was too early for Hazel to have any life-changing revelations about family and stability, but it certainly felt good to enjoy this small victory of her daughter getting excited about their new home.

Fullmer took the bowl from his sister. "Poppy took me fishing at the lake for a little while. Poppy caught—"

"One, two, three—" Hazel was mimicking her brother's counting habit between bites of her roll.

"He caught seven fish," Fullmer announced.

Hazel dropped her roll and turned to her mom, incredulous. "He's not gonna count 'em?"

"He caught seven fish," Lizzie repeated. She was grinning. Fullmer wasn't going to count them.

"Hancock," Bill prompted. "It's your turn. Grab some grub."

Fullmer passed Lizzie the bowl, and she took a soft, white roll from off the top. She held it in her hands, letting it warm her fingertips. Fullmer wasn't going to count the fish.

"Grace Barker told me that the Baron is putting on *Fiddler on the Roof*." The words were coming out of her mouth before she knew she was saying them.

Nora's eyebrows went up. "Really?" she asked. "And are you—"

"No, no." Lizzie answered, grounding herself once more. Where had her head been a moment ago?

"Are you gonna what?" Caroline piped up, taking the bowl from Lizzie to go next.

"Going to audition," Nora answered.

"Audition?" Caroline was puzzled.

"Back in high school, your Aunt Lizzie was quite the actress. All-County, right, Hancock?" Bill asked.

"All-State," Lizzie corrected, her voice quiet.

"She was really somethin'," Nora commented, folding her arms and looking back on some long ago moment. "She was always singing songs and making up choreography. She was the Drama Club president our senior year. Oh! And she founded that puppetry group with David Flannery—"

"It was all a long time ago," Lizzie said. "I haven't been on stage in a hot minute. I'd probably just embarrass myself if I went to the audition."

"*What* is an audition?" Caroline crushed her roll in an angry fist, insistent.

"Simmer down, child," said Poppy, winking at her as he

chucked his napkin at her face. Caroline broke into a fit of giggles.

"An audition is a sort of tryout. It's where you sing a little song or act a little scene, and if they like it, they put you in a play." The kids were all focused in on Nora, who doled out her wisdom like a sage. "Lizzie went on tons of 'em when she first moved out to New York. She was always calling me after, all giddy—"

"All giddy and naïve." Lizzie reached across the table and grabbed the bottle of wine, pouring herself an extra tall glass. It was too bitter.

"Mama, you never sing for us," Hazel whined.

"To be fair, you won't let me sing lullabies anymore. You just tell me to get out of your room already so that you can write in your diary." Lizzie teased.

"She was really good," Bill commented. "I always poked fun at Aunt Lizzie for being too nerdy, but she actually made drama pretty cool for a while. A big group of us would go to all her shows."

Nora's face lit up. "Lizzie! You should sing for us now!"

Lizzie knocked back a long swig of the wine. "I'm sorry, who gets the rolls next?"

"Sing!" Hazel banged an enthusiastic fist on the table.

"No one wants to hear that," Lizzie said.

"SING!" Nora joined the urging.

"Pass." She answered.

"*Start spreadin' the news.*"

The family quit talking as Poppy's voice filled the air. It was caramel smooth, with each note bright and clear. There was something older to his sound, something that went beyond his numeric age. Frank Sinatra's iconic jazz lyrics came out sounding exactly as they would have been intended, strong and confident and brassy.

"*I'm leavin' today.*" Lizzie was shocked to hear Fullmer's quiet voice joining in the verse. A small smile pulled at his lips and he sang out. "*I want to be a part of it. New York, New York.*"

Sighing a bit but smiling, Lizzie raised her own voice. "*These vagabond shoes,*" Bill started to hoot and holler as Lizzie's voice rounded out the trio. "*Are longing to stray. Right through the very heart of it—*"

The whole room swelled with sound as Nora and Bill took up the song. "*New York, New Yooooork!*"

Poppy and Fullmer went quiet, as if on cue. Lizzie cleared her throat. "*I want to wake up in a city that doesn't sleep—*"

As she carried on the song, Lizzie was surprised to find that she remembered every word. The phrases came to her lips before she could even think of them, erupting as though they had lain dormant, waiting for ages to be released. She closed her eyes, letting the music carry her, feeling the unplayed melody resonating in her bones.

When she finished the song, she opened her eyes once more. Her kids sat quiet, expectant. And then, in perfect time, they erupted into cheers together. The whole table was cheering, with Bill leading a rousing chant of "Lizzie! Lizzie!"

She could feel the blush staining her cheeks. She looked down at her lap, fidgeting with her napkin. Still, she couldn't help but smile.

"Well," Nora said as the cheering calmed down. "It's a shame that you won't be going to that audition then, Lizzie. Who was next to have a roll?"

"M-hm," Lizzie answered, nodding. "Maybe next time." Her feet betrayed her, tapping out choreography under the dinner table.

CHAPTER 6

*T*here was fog everywhere. Pressing. Insistent. It puffed from a fog machine, a dusty, rusted old thing that sat behind the red curtain and pumped out a blanket of heavy mist that cut through the stage lights to form a thick cloud around Lizzie's body.

She could barely see the audience through the fog, their dark outlines shifting as individual forms turned to whisper to one another. She hated that she couldn't hear what they were saying.

This was a theater she was familiar with. She'd been on auditions here a thousand times, but never got far enough in the process to be singing alone on stage. Lizzie felt the nerves stab into her stomach all at once, churning her insides until she wasn't sure she could stand anymore.

"Hey!" a quiet voice whispered to her from behind the curtain. She turned but couldn't see the source. "You don't have to do this. They can't see you through the fog. Duck back here, there's a stage door!"

Lizzie turned back to the audience. He was right. She couldn't see their faces, but she felt so sure that she could just step off stage *and no one would notice. She'd be fine. She started to step toward the voice.*

Someone was clapping. She turned back, quick, straining her eyes to find the source. They were in the crowd, near the front. She put her hand to her forehead, shielding herself from the stage lights.

"You got this!" A man in the audience called to her. He clapped louder and started to cheer.

The fog started to clear. She could see the front row now, empty save for two seats. Hazel and Fullmer. They were dressed to the nines, looking better than Lizzie had ever been able to afford to dress them. They clapped and stood to cheer. "Sing for us, Mom!"

Something swelled inside of her. Lizzie stepped forward, hesitant, but gaining momentum with each clap. The man in the crowd called out again. "You can do this!" Lizzie opened her mouth, feeling her breath build inside her belly.

All at once, the lights cut on, blinding her.

"Follow me!" The voice called from behind the curtain.

Lizzie figured that a dime store psychologist would have been able to crack the code of her pre-audition dream.

All the symbols were so painfully obvious. She'd been performing in the same rundown theater she'd been out to for so many auditions when she'd first come to New York City. It was a crap hole, roach infested with homeless people camping out front and only a five-dollar entrance fee. But she hadn't been able to break into the ensemble there, had she? She'd always never been *quite* good enough, *quite* practiced enough. She'd lasted auditions there for a whopping one month before she'd learned she was pregnant with the kids. No one was going to cast a pregnant woman in *Thoroughly Modern Millie*. She'd moved to Jersey, the only place where she could find some good money and a cheap apartment, living alone, dejected, and feeling too stupid to reach out to the father.

And as for the voices, at least there was some variation there. Usually her inner monologue was in her own voice, which got a bit boring. Thanks, psyche, for shaking things up a bit.

Grace Barker had given Lizzie a ride to the theater, and the dream had been playing on repeat at the back of her mind the whole way over. She hadn't even noticed that they'd pulled into the parking lot until there it was, the red brick Baron, looming over her in all its faded glory. Grace had launched into a recent history of the theater and its current renovations while Lizzie scooped up her things and swallowed down the dream as far as it would go.

Her stomach took that now-familiar icy tumble. Was she sure she wanted to do this? She'd resisted coming back to Warner Robins for so long: was she just going to jump right back into the theater life she used to live as soon as one old friend convinced her to stick around for a minute? Lizzie took a step back, second-guessing her decision. It wasn't too late to tell Grace that she would be too busy with her nanny job or her kids or—

"You comin'?" Grace looked at her, expectant.

"Sure thing." Lizzie smiled at Grace but winced as soon as she turned her back. Curse her engrained need to be agreeable. She braved the threshold, following Grace into the Baron.

She was surprised at how many people she saw in the lobby. An eclectic group of actors were gathered in a circle nearby, pounding out a rather intense vocal warm-up.

"Twilight, New Moon, Eclipse, and Breaking Dawn. *Midnight Sun!*"

She laughed, surprising herself. Grace grinned, too.

"Yeah," Her friend commented. "Vocal warm-ups have changed for the funnier since we were in high school Thespians. I do a killer rendition of 'lips, teeth, tip of the tongue' if you wanna go old school with me."

"Thanks, but I think I need to check out the bathroom first," Lizzie replied, shrugging out of her jacket to reveal her leotard underneath.

"Down the hall and on the right," Grace directed, pulling off her sweats and slipping on a gaudy pair of magenta leg warmers. "They've got those fancy dryers!" Lizzie left her friend in the lobby, picking her way through the crowds of stretching and flexing auditioners to make her way to the ladies' room.

The privacy of the hallway brought near instant relief. Lizzie felt her shoulder relax instinctively and a long breath expelled that she hadn't even realized she'd been holding. The hallway was just as she remembered it from a lifetime of summers spent at drama day camp. On the walls balanced refined sconces, their light fixtures clouded with dust but still giving off that hazy gleam Lizzie had always associated with the tension and glamour of live theater. The walls were crushed velvet red, and Lizzie ran her fingertips along their soft texture, letting the familiarity of the touch relax her. No bathroom, though. She pressed on down the hall until a black door finally revealed itself. She pushed it open.

"Oof!"

"Oh, God!"

Papers scattered everywhere. The door hadn't been the bathroom after all, and Lizzie had smacked into a very irritated employee who was making his way out from backstage, clearly balancing a large stack of resumes and headshots. Or at least, he *was* balancing the stack.

Lizzie collapsed to her hands and knees, scrambling to pick up glossy photos. The panic from before was back, compounded by her embarrassment. The man was down on his knees, too, trying his best to un-crumble a resume she had stepped on. "I'm so sorry!" she cried. "I was looking for the bathroom."

The man looked up at her, his brow creased with frustration. He was tall and broad, practically hulking even bent over the way that he was. He certainly didn't look like the Baron Theater employees of Lizzie's youth, with a trim, chestnut beard and heavy eyebrows that almost obscured his green eyes. The only things that separated him from her mental image of a mountain man was his red wool Mr. Rogers cardigan, which he had pushed up to his elbows, revealing a full, colorful sleeve of tattoos.

"You're in the wrong hall," he said. He nudged his elbow to his right, pointing her the other direction, and busied himself once more with picking up the papers.

"Let me help you finish picking these up," she said. "It's the least I can do."

"I'm fine." He waved her off, not bothering to look up.

She stood, awkward and uncomfortable, brushing herself off before heading off to find the bathroom.

When she returned to the lobby, a young girl was standing at the theater doors, calling for everyone to head out into the audience seats.

"Oh Lord," Grace muttered. "I hate the anticipation. Gets me every time!" She hooked her arm through Lizzie's and showed her up to the top row of seats, where an eclectic group of auditioners sat together.

"Hey, y'all," Grace called, waving. "I'm sure everyone remembers—"

"Lizzie Hancock? It can't be!" Lizzie was crushed in a

massive bear hug. Clint Stone stood before her, aggressively eyeballing every inch of her from head to toe. She was surprised to see his signature blonde shag hair cut from high school slicked back into a sophisticated sweep and the barest hint of rouge on his pale cheeks. "You haven't changed a stitch."

"You have!" Lizzie gushed, the words coming out before she had time to overthink them. "I'd call it a glow up, but you were always handsome."

"We can call it what it is, my love. I got the heck out of Redneck Nowhere for a little while and learned that there were more stores for clothing than Wal-Mart and Target."

Lizzie grinned. "You still have the sense of humor that I remember."

"Razor sharp." He winked.

Lizzie was surprised at how comfortable the quick introduction had made her feel. The vice on her chest had loosened. She'd expected more embarrassment, more awkwardness. This was surprisingly... bearable.

"It's my turn!" Ashley Walker stood to hug Lizzie next. Always the quirky, goofball side character in high school, the last decade had softened her strangeness and left her looking put together and mature. She wore her hair in a long, curled mane instead of her braided pigtails, and the checkered jacket she'd clung to for four years had been replaced by a smart, tailored coat she was taking off to reveal her audition wear. "I can't believe you're here! What has it been—"

"Ten years," Clint answered, one eyebrow cocked. "You know the reunion ain't til May, right?"

"I can still count," Lizzie laughed. "I'm, uh ... I'm living over at Nora Grant's house." Ah. There was the embarrassment she'd been expecting.

"Wait, you don't have your own place?" Ashley asked.

The stage lights began to dim, and the auditioners started to quiet down. The group took their seats and Grace bent over in front of Lizzie, more than ready to provide details about her life. "Two kids—twins!—no husband and no reason not to spend every wakin' moment livin' and breathin' drama with us. She'll be here for the foreseeable future."

"Ooh, you'll have to start coming to our margarita nights at Tequila's!" Ashley squealed.

The man from the hallway was walking out onto the stage, the stack of headshots and resumes piled into a neat stack once more. Now his red cardigan was gone, revealing the theater's more traditional backstage attire of black jeans under a fitted black t-shirt. His tattoos extended even farther than Lizzie had thought, wrapping their way up tight muscles to hide somewhere beneath his sleeves.

"Welcome to the Baron."

The auditioners erupted into cheers. The man onstage smiled and waved one hand, indicating the need for quiet. "I'm glad you could all make it. I'll be your director for this year's production of *Fiddler on the Roof*."

"Oh God, no." Lizzie sank down into her seat, covering her red face. "I ran into this guy in the hall. Made the worst possible impression."

Grace leaned towards her, excited once more. "You didn't tell me you already ran into David Flannery!"

"*What?*" Lizzie jerked forward in her chair, straining her eyes to see better. "That's David Flannery?"

She couldn't believe it. How had she not recognized him? She and David had been best friends in high school, their relationship rivaling that of hers with Nora. He had been her confidant and trusted advisor, the one she turned to for everything.

But he'd been... *not* this guy. David Flannery was tall, but soft and chubby. He had permanent smiling cheeks, the kind of face that put everyone at ease. He was funny and easy-going, fitting in with everyone he met. He'd worn geeky Broadway shirts and had a terrible, long haircut and knew an Oscar Wilde quote for every situation, and he was a far cry from the chiseled Brawny man that Lizzie had accosted in the hallway.

She felt her face turn an even deeper red as she thought back to their last meeting. David had always cared for Lizzie. For the longest time, she had thought of him as a brother until that last night she was in Warner Robins. Graduation night. He'd put it all on the line. And she... well, maybe Lizzie had an even worse chance at getting a role in his production than she had initially thought. She shook her head fiercely, banishing the memory back to the dark corner of her mind where it belonged.

"Now *that's* your glow-up, baby." Clint muttered. He growled playfully, sending Ashley and Grace into a fit of giggles.

"We went out once," Ashley mused. "Now I both thank and curse God for not letting us make it to a second date. I never would have known what to do with that body."

"This is his place now." Grace whispered to Lizzie. "He's been runnin' it for years. Bought it off Ole Man Stark. He started a bunch of renovations. I told you that, right? I'm sure I told you that."

Lizzie shook her head no, her stomach twisting inside of her.

David pulled a resume out of his stack and waved it for the audience. "When I call your name, come on down, give the pianist your music, and show us what you got. Keep it under 20 bars, people. We don't want to hear the entirety of *Old Man River* again, Matthew." He gestured to an older man in the front row, and the audience lit up with laughter. "After, we'll do a quick dance audition, and we'll call you if you're coming in for callbacks."

A tall blonde woman, dressed in black like David, walked onto the stage, one hand to her face to shield her from the stage lights. "Margo will take your music and play for you," David said, putting a hand on the pianist's back to guide her forward. Lizzie felt her throat tighten. Margo waved to the audience before giving David's hand a quick squeeze and slipping behind the piano. He pulled the first resume off the stack. "Clint Stone, you're up!"

Beaming, Clint strutted down the audience stairs to the stage below. He blew a big kiss and winked up at Lizzie and their friends before putting a hand on his hip. "Count me in, Margo."

After Clint's rousing rendition of "Giants in the Sky," the call list went on. Lizzie felt herself sliding further down in her seat as she saw familiar face after familiar face taking the stage. Was her entire high school drama class still living and performing in Warner Robins? Did no one but her try to leave? She couldn't help but feel silly. She was the one who took a chance, actually tried to put herself out there, but sitting here amongst the crowd of mediocrity, she felt more than ever like she'd failed on an epic scale.

"Lizzie Hancock!"

She sat back up. It was surreal to hear her name coming from David Flannery once more. She spied him down in the front row. He wasn't looking up at her, instead burying his head in her resume. Lizzie felt her cheeks burn as she wondered if he was taking note of its remarkable lack of Broadway credits.

"Lizzie, *go!*" Grace's pointy elbows were bruising her side as she pushed.

Lizzie stumbled to her feet, loudly dropping her binder of sheet music. The group sitting in front of her turned, surprised, and she gave an awkward wave as she sent up one last desperate plea to the theater gods that all these people from high school would have somehow magically forgotten her face and name.

She took the stairs slowly, focusing on her breathing. When she reached the stage, she shuffled over to Margo the pianist, who flashed a gleaming white smile at her before whispering, "Where do you want me to start?"

"I have it marked." Still looking at the floor, Lizzie walked to the center of the stage.

You got this.

She looked up. Margo had started playing her in. Lizzie looked up, letting her vision go out of focus so that the audience blended in with the stage lights. She cleared her throat and started in on the lyrics of *Les Misérables's* "On My Own."

Somehow, this felt more like a dream than the vision that had been playing in her head on repeat. The notes came out of Lizzie's mouth sounding foreign and strange, but also delicate and beautiful. For twenty blissful bars, she was a street urchin, pining for a life that she couldn't have. The audience was there, but it wasn't there. It had melted into that familiar hazy glow, pressing in on her, warm and comfortable. She had forgotten how good this felt. A sense of desperate urgency penetrated each note she sang, as she leaned into the melody and let it wash over her. She wanted to—

"Thank you, that's enough!"

Lizzie blinked. She was back in the Baron, standing alone on the stage. She could see David Flannery in the front row. He still wasn't looking at her. She wondered if he had at all.

The audience broke out into claps. Lizzie was jarred, shielding her eyes to look out into the sea of faces. People were standing. She could make out Grace, Ashley, and Clint at the back, who were waving their jackets over their heads. Clint wolf-whistled.

She smiled. For the first moment in all her time back in Warner Robins, she felt the first fleeting feelings of calm. She was authentic and relaxed. Maybe she'd failed in New York. But she was still in the game.

CHAPTER 7

*L*izzie could smell the cigarette smoke before she could see it.

She locked her borrowed car behind her and slipped on a thick, woolen cardigan she'd stashed on the front seat. It wasn't cold. Certainly not New Jersey cold, that is. But the Georgia air was sharp and moist, cutting through her audition clothes to nibble her skin, uncharacteristic of the pressing, humid Indian summers she recalled from her youth. Lizzie let herself around the back of the house, the deck light on once more.

Nora stood at the railing, eyes closed as she inhaled, thin cigarette pinched with care between her first three fingers. In a sudden wind, her dark hair whipped around in a perfect halo. The smoke blew toward Lizzie once more, tickling her lungs.

"That stuff'll kill you, ya know." She laughed through a cough as she took the steps up the deck to stand next to her friend.

Nora coughed, too, as though it were contagious. She

half-smiled, bringing the cigarette back to her lips to take another meaningful drag. "You sound like my husband."

"And your dad, and your friends, and every doctor who treated your mom for lung cancer before she passed." Lizzie pulled her cardigan tighter and nuzzled up against her friend's warm body.

"I'm sucking the marrow out of life. Doing it all. You should try it sometime." Nora's eyes were fixed on a spot in the distance, somewhere where the manicured lawn gave way to untamed pine trees and persistent honeysuckle.

Maybe Nora had changed a little from when Lizzie had seen her last. Here she was, this brilliant, conscientious doctor who had graduated at the top of her class and she was ... smoking? Lizzie couldn't help but wonder if there was more to the story here. Nora had seen how her own mother had suffered from lung cancer. In fact, she knew the consequences better than anyone else. Lizzie shuddered at a sudden dark memory from their high school years. These were the kinds of things in Warner Robins that she'd been reluctant to come home to.

Nora took one more drag and, without breaking her distant stare, offered the cigarette to Lizzie with a casual flick of the wrist. "You want a hit?" She chuckled, her gaze softening around the corners of her eyes. It was a statement more than a question.

"No way," Lizzie answered, opting to settle her head in on Nora's shoulder instead. "You're a bad influence on me," she joked. She couldn't help it; she breathed in the smell deeply, feeling a bit like a teenager once more.

"I know." Nora grinned, finally breaking away to pull her friend close and take her in. She pulled back just as fast, recoiling. "Lord, Lizzie, you're sweating like a whore in church!"

"I was nervous! Geez!" Lizzie passed back the cigarette and crossed her arms against the wind. "It has been an embarrassingly long time since I last auditioned for something."

"How did it go?" Nora's eyes lit up with interest as she crossed the deck, settling into a weathered lawn chair.

"It was—" Lizzie paused the recycled complaint she felt welling on her tongue. Was she really that used to things going badly? "... I think I killed it."

"Shut up! Praise Jesus." Nora crossed her legs underneath her body, leaning forward eagerly. "Give me all the details."

"It's not like it was that exciting," she started. "I sang *Les Mis*—"

"It always was your best."

"Obviously. I hit my notes, never strained. Another girl sang Fantine's song, but that wasn't a big deal—" Once Lizzie started in, the words bubbled up inside her, rushing all at once to be released. Giddiness gripped her, and she spilled everything, every tiny detail, every perfect, vibrating moment that had been searing into her brain since the morning.

"Clint and Ashley were there—"

"Lord, have you seen his hair? He looks so much more like himself since he came out."

"That cut must have cost fifty dollars!"

"At least!"

"Anyway, they were incredible," Lizzie continued. "I can't believe I wrote them off as amateur back in high school."

Nora snorted. "Back in high school, you wrote off everyone in theater as amateur."

"I was so full of it," Lizzie groaned and slid into the deck chair next to Nora. "If only I could see myself in ten years, greased up serving burgers at a diner because I couldn't hack it on Broadway. Maybe I would have been more humble."

Nora smacked Lizzie on the arm. "Don't do that. Don't rewrite history. How was the Baron? We haven't been over there since before the remodel." She offered Lizzie the cigarette once more, but Lizzie waved her off again, giggling.

"It's *unreal*," she moaned to Nora. "It's looking so good." She paused, examining the dying cigarette between her friend's fingers. "I thought I remember you preferring something stronger than cigarettes back in the day."

"Elizabeth Hancock, I am a doctor."

"And a high school stoner, as I recall," Lizzie winked.

Nora shot her a wry grin. "Alright, so maybe I've got something medicinal upstairs."

Cigarettes and weed? Lizzie couldn't pin this new Nora down. She wondered how much Bill knew about his wife's extracurriculars.

"Mmm, I'll have to raid your bedroom later." Lizzie laughed. "You should seriously go check out the Baron. It's amazing, like something out of New York. All red velvet and shiny brass and stuff. Must have cost a fortune to hire out."

"Not really," Nora took another drag on the cigarette. "David Flannery has been doing it all himself with donations from the patrons."

"Hmm." Lizzie pulled her cardigan tighter.

"What?" Nora asked, one eyebrow cocked. "You have feelings about Clint's fifty dollar haircut but not about Chris Hemsworth Junior?"

"He looked great." She agreed. "Good for him."

"Yeah," Nora laughed. "*Great* for him. I'm surprised you recognized him at all."

"I didn't," Lizzie found herself shaking her head involuntarily. "He must have lost—"

"Sixty pounds. I'm one of the only doctors in town, remember? I'm privy to the little details." Nora winked. "He changed after high school. Got in shape, grew the beard. Bought the Baron. Outside of the obvious candidates, he might be the most eligible bachelor from here to Macon."

"That's great."

Nora sat up, folding her arms and shooting her friend a look. "Come on, you must have reached out to him at least once. You were best friends."

"You and I are best friends," Lizzie corrected.

"You and I are sisters. David always had your back."

Lizzie groaned and slouched down into her seat. She pulled the cardigan up over her face. "God, this *town*."

"Did you have a fight or something? You've never told me."

"It's ancient history." Lizzie stood up suddenly, heading for the back door. The excitement of the morning's audition had pushed back her desire to run as far from Warner Robins as her feet could carry her, but now she was being reminded why she'd avoided her home for so long. Nora grabbed her arm, pulling her back.

"It's ancient history," she agreed. "But it still happened. *We* still happened. Warner Robins is part of you. You can't ignore that."

"Maybe I shouldn't have come back after all," Lizzie snapped, pulling her hand back. "This is why I never visit. You can't walk into Walmart without running into the entire football team from high school. I cross city lines and suddenly I'm plunged back into high school drama, friendships—"

"Is it really so bad to have friends?" Nora's eyes were

dark and pleading. "Is it so bad to have people who care about what happens to you and want to be around you..." She trailed off, and once more her gaze disappeared to that far-off point behind Lizzie, deep in the tangles of the dark thicket.

Lizzie sighed and sat down once more. She took the cigarette from Nora, flicking it to the ground and stamping it out. She gathered her friend's hands in her own, squeezing them.

"Listen, Nora. Maybe staying here isn't the best idea." Lizzie cleared her throat. "I love our friendship. Really, I do. And it was good to see Clint and Ashley and even Glow-Up Ken Doll David Flannery and get a little window into what life is like on the other side. But, all this—I'm being silly. I made my choice a long time ago. Ten years ago, before I even knew I was pregnant or a talentless hack—"

Lizzie paused. She'd never had this conversation out loud before. It had played a million times over in her head, echoing around in there, reverberating until it became something strong and formidable and haunting. Time in the dark and quiet had given it power over her. She'd confirmed the idea over and over again that things were just the way that they were, and there was no use in trying to change them. Lizzie was powerless to her own fate, destined to work at the Starshine and barely hack together a life for her children, doing it all on her own and far, far away from the world she had once called home.

Saying the words out loud, though... some curse had been broken. They'd been weakened, exposed in the fading light of a cool Georgia evening. They appeared stark and naked before her, suddenly exposed for the lie that they were.

"Lizzie," Nora started, giving her hands a squeeze.

"There's no rule that says you aren't allowed to change your mind."

Sutton Foster's *Anything Goes* cut through the heavy air between them.

"God, it's my phone. Sorry." Lizzie let go of Nora's hands, fumbling in her pocket to retrieve the device. BARON flashed across the screen. "It's the theater," she said, her eyes going wide. The phone vibrated again.

"Lord, woman! Pick it up before my nerves make me break out another cigarette!"

"Uh, hello?" Lizzie held the phone to her ear. She was surprised to find that she was shaking.

"Elizabeth? It's Margo, from the Baron."

"Yeah, hey! How are you?" Lizzie could tell that she was talking too fast.

Margo's laugh was bubbly and bright on the other end. "I'm good, thanks. I was calling about the auditions—"

"Yeah, yeah, yeah. The auditions." Nora was mouthing "*Well?*" "Thanks for letting me come out. It was kind of a last-minute thing. I'm sure you prefer to see our music ahead of time—"

"No, it's fine." Margo laughed again. "We'd like to offer you a role."

"A ... role." Nora was mouthing questions again, and Lizzie batted her away with one hand. She pressed the phone tighter to her ear and walked to the other end of the deck. Her stomach was a tight knot, threatening to burst up and out from her mouth at any moment. "Which—"

"How would you feel about Golde, Tevye's wife?" Margo asked. "She's probably lead female, with quite a few musical numbers. I was very impressed with your singing, though, and some of our usual performers vouched for your acting, so we think that you're up for it. What do you think?"

"Holy shit."

"Excuse me?" Margo's soft Southern voice sounded genuinely surprised at the profanity.

"Oh, God, sorry!" Lizzie said. Nora smacked Lizzie on the back of the head, laughed, and pulled out her cigarette pack to produce another smoke. She lit it and puffed with nervous anticipation. "It's just... you're sure you meant to call me?"

"Do you want the role, Liz?"

"Obviously!" Lizzie's voice erupted in a full shout. She clasped a quick hand over her mouth, surprised by the outburst. Nora cackled, slapping a hand to her own mouth to cover the sound. "I mean, that sounds great. I'd love to accept the role."

Margo laughed again, saccharine sweet. "First rehearsal is on Monday at six. Come in comfortable clothes. And bring that enthusiasm. I like it."

"Thank you!" Lizzie shut off her phone. Her eyes were transfixed on the bright, glowing screen.

"Well?" Nora pulled her back to reality as she gestured her excited question. "What's the verdict?"

"I'm the lead. I landed a lead."

"Hmm," Nora said. She smiled and slipped back into her deck chair. "Sounds like a good reason for another smoke to me. And maybe a good reason to stick around for a while after all."

"Hmm," Lizzie muttered. She settled into her own chair and found her eyes drifting off to that same unseen spot in the darkness where Nora had been looking before.

CHAPTER 8

"*L*ord, a tight five ain't time enough to pull down yer pants to piss much less time enough to chug a coffee."

"Grace Barker," Clint complained, his voice curt but patient. "You know I've been wanting to get over to this coffee shop ever since it opened. If we don't support Warner Robins small business culture—"

"*It will disappear before our eyes,*" Grace and Ashley chanted in unison, bursting into a fit of giggles.

Clint rolled his eyes, but smiled. He flung his bag over his shoulder. "You coming, Lizzie? David's tight fives always turn into tight tens, anyway. We'll have plenty of time to pick up a mocha before rehearsal gets back."

"Yeah," Lizzie replied. "Count me in."

She picked up her own bag and swung it over her shoulder, enjoying the familiar weight of it. Damp, frizzing curls clung to the sides of her cheeks in baths of sweat. Her pants hung loose around her hips from being stretched out in dance practice. Her body felt sore and strong, pulsing with an energy that hadn't been called upon in years. She relished the feeling. Through the nerves that persisted and the sense of embarrassment that still clouded her mind, Lizzie could feel it: she was finally starting to settle in here. A little theater familiarity went a long way.

Lizzie's days were spent shuffling kids between school and extracurriculars, keeping up the house, and bringing Poppy, Bill, and Nora whatever lunch item or fishing gear they may have forgotten on their way out the door in the morning. It was tough work, but nothing that a mother to twins wasn't fully prepared for. Unfortunately, it was boring and lonely. Lizzie began to look to *Fiddler* as her escape from responsibility. After an entire adulthood spent slaving behind the counter of a diner and losing hair over her kids' well-being, it turned out that she enjoyed the little break. Her nights had become her own, and she looked forward to trading off the kids to Poppy in the evenings more than she could have ever anticipated.

Rehearsal had begun in full force. The entire cast had shown up at the Baron in their various hoodies and jazz shoes, eager to limber up and get to work. The first hour would be spent with Margo slaving furiously at the piano, matching David's intense, focused directions beat for beat. The five-minute coffee break would be well deserved.

Clint led the group out of the theater and across the street. They walked a road thick with cherry blossom trees, their limbs no longer heavy and full with soft pink flowers, but instead guarding the group's journey with thin, sharp arms that bore brilliant shades of red and orange. The coffee shop, a cozy little place with faded white brick and a repurposed awning, sat on a corner, inviting them in with decadent smells of rich coffee and pastries.

"Thanks in advance for ruining my diet, Clint," Ashley laughed, pulling open the door and held it for her friends.

The café was packed. Every nook and cranny was filled with bodies, from businessmen grabbing the fuel for a late night at the office to soccer moms gossiping over a cup while their kids had practice. The small group got in at the back of the lengthy line and Lizzie had to stand on her tiptoes to see the menu board.

"Is that a lavender latte I see up there, Clint?" She was squinting and hopping.

"Can't tell," he muttered, his scrunched-up face indicating that his own eyes were straining.

"Go up and look for yourself," Ashley chimed in. "We'll beat back anyone who tries to gun for your spot in line."

Lizzie flashed a grateful smile and let herself out of the line to weave her way through bodies up to the front. In the middle of such masses, the thick, sweet air seemed to choke her. "Excuse me," she murmured, waving a hand at strangers to push her way through. A tall man in a gray suit was her last roadblock to the registers.

"Sir, can I just—"

"Gracious!"

The man had spun around at her call, knocking into her with three full to-go cups. Coffee washed over Lizzie's shirt, drowning her in shades of frothy browns and lilacs.

"Ugh," she groaned, pulling the sopping fabric away from her abdomen. "Well, that burns a bit. I guess they did have the lavender latte after all. I have got to stop running into people this way."

"It's nothing," the man replied. He grabbed some napkins off the counter and got down to wipe up the floor. "Please, ma'am, don't worry yourself—"

He stopped short. Lizzie finished wringing out her shirt and looked down.

"Ellis?"

"Elizabeth. You look—"

Lizzie felt her face flush. In an instant, she could see herself from outside her own body, soaked in coffee, sweaty from rehearsal, and wearing sweatpants borrowed from her best friend's husband. "...Wet?"

"Incredible. You haven't aged a day."

Ellis Clarke pushed up from his spot on the floor. Lizzie's ex-boyfriend. Lizzie's *only* ex-boyfriend.

He was tall, towering really. Lizzie could remember this from when they were together in high school, but it was one thing to recall a detail like this in her mind's eye and another to see it once more in person. He was at least 6'3" and built like a football player. Which he had been, in fact. For the months after she left Warner Robins, Lizzie could remember obsessively combing the papers online for word of how he'd played at UGA. He was a rockstar. A god. And six years after college, Ellis Clarke still had the body to prove it.

His face had changed, though. Bright, boyish eyes were now deep blue wells under unnerving, thick blonde eyebrows. His smile at Lizzie was broad and curious, the kind of expression that compelled its subject to speak despite any reservations. She could feel that compulsion now, as she stammered to respond to his compliment.

"I'm wearing coffee-stained men's sweatpants." Did she just describe her sweaty outfit? No quirky retort?

"And, just like in high school, you make it a *look*," Ellis laughed, a deep, hearty sound that gave Lizzie a rush at the back of her head. "It's amazing to see you. What are you doing in town? It's got to have been—"

"A decade," she finished, nodding. "We're ... I ... um, I'm staying with Nora. She gave me a job."

"And Warner Robins is better off for it. God," he breathed. "Elizabeth Hancock..."

It was shocking how quickly he transported her back to another time in her life. Seeing him now, hearing the soft, reverent way he said her name with his slow, Southern drawl ... it was difficult to remember the complicated reasons why things hadn't worked out between them the first time around. Ellis Clarke's high school charisma had only intensified with time, especially the way that his earnest, genuine compliments could make Lizzie feel like she was the only girl in the world who merited such care and attention. Whatever it was, he had it going on. Lizzie could feel her face getting redder by the minute.

Still, there was something about him that put Lizzie on edge. She felt more than self-conscious around him; she felt skittish. Apprehensive? Nervous? It was a difficult feeling to put into words.

She had thought about him a million times since high school, replaying the last days she had seen him. In fact, she'd replayed the memories so much that they were starting to distort and take on a new life of their own. They had morphed into strange, miscolored versions of the way things really were. Sometimes, she convinced herself that Ellis was a monster for ending things with her the way that he did. Other times, she was the one who deserved all the blame. Historically, thinking about their relationship had ended in confusion and a sick feeling for Lizzie.

Now, though, seeing Ellis standing in front of her looking so open and so deliciously handsome and charming... It was hard to imagine how she had ever envisioned him as a bad guy at all. Lizzie could feel her face getting redder by the minute.

"Lizzie, did they have the lavender latte?" Ashley was

tapping Lizzie on the shoulder. The group had made their way to the front of the line. She blushed at the sight of Ellis Clarke. "Oh, hi, Ellis. How's it going?"

Grace and Clint turned around and caught sight of him, too. "Well, I'm definitely orderin' off menu," murmured Grace with a smile. Clint elbowed her.

"The law firm is still kicking. Thanks for asking. I was just about to bring back the late-night coffee order for the crew when I ran into Lizzie here."

Lizzie could feel her face flush with renewed embarrassment. "I'm so sorry, I'm wearing your order. Let me buy you some new drinks."

Ellis put a hand up to stop her from reaching for her wallet and produced a sleek black billfold of his own. "Nonsense," he said. "It's me who owes you a new shirt. And can I buy you all coffee as well? It's the least I can do after making a scene for poor Mrs. Hancock here."

"It's Miss." Grace volunteered the information in a loud voice, winking at the group when she thought Ellis wasn't looking anymore. *Oh God.* "We're just fine without the help. But yer a gent for offerin'. Why don't you just help clean our Lizzie off so she can get back to rehearsal?"

"Rehearsal?" Ellis' eyes were wide and curious as he put a hand to the small of Lizzie's back and whisked her out of the coffee shop. "There's no way I'm coming between Lizzie and a theater. We've gotta get you back. I've got my workout clothes in my car if you want something. Or I can run down the street really fast. There's a Banana Republic—"

"The workout shirt is fine." Lizzie assured him. "I'm sure anything is an improvement on the grungy clothes I was wearing before."

Ellis led her over to a black Lexus parked off to the side of the café. He opened the side door and bent over to fish around in his backseat. Grinning, he produced a faded crimson Warner Robins High School Football Boosters t-shirt. "It probably smells a bit like the mountains of Chick-Fil-A that have been piling up in my backseat all week. Forgive me."

"I ... um ..." Lizzie fumbled to find a way to put the shirt on and finally settled for pulling it over head and awkwardly retrieving her coffee-stained blouse through the armhole. "Thank you, Ellis." Her face was hot with a blush. "Well, I have to be getting back, I've been gone for way too long."

"Ugh, me too," he groaned and checked the time on his cell phone. "I hate putting in these awful hours lately, but I've been saving for a bigger place, somewhere I could really grow into. You know how it is. Adulting is the worst." He laughed.

She wondered what his place looked like now. Were they really at the stage of life when a young man would trade in the bachelor pad for a family home? The butterflies in her tummy returned once more. The Ellis that she'd known back in high school was fun and carefree, unworried about preparing for the future or taking care of someone else. This new version of the boy she thought she remembered did things to her.

She couldn't stop herself. Her mind drifted off to the forbidden fantasy in which she stopped slaving away and had her own home to grow into. A place with individual rooms for both of her children. Her own privacy. It was a fantasy more tempting and secret than even the thoughts she had late at night, when she was all alone in the dark... thoughts about men very much like Ellis Clarke...

Lizzie hid her reddening face once more by checking her watch. Yikes. She was definitely going to be running behind.

"Thanks for the dry clothing," she said. She cleared her throat. "It was great to see you, Ellis."

She started to wave and step away, but he put a hand on her arm. "Only thing is... I still owe you a coffee. Think you can spare a minute for me tomorrow night?"

"I owe *you* coffee, remember? For your whole firm."

"Let's just call it even by you coming out with me." He grinned.

Lizzie shuffled, hoping desperately that the fading light would disguise how red she was getting. She was torn. Ellis was so easy-going and inviting, but also someone that she'd spent a lot of time trying to get over. What she really wanted was time away from the butterflies in her stomach to think through how she really felt. But she couldn't exactly say no, could she? Making anything that remotely resembled a *scene* went against her every instinct to disappear into the background of Warner Robins. Ellis was still smiling at her. Maybe she could say yes now and sort through her feelings later?

"I suppose one cup wouldn't be the worse thing in the world," she said.

He reached out and squeezed her hand. She felt her breath catch in her throat and looked away, checking her watch. Lizzie winced. "I think my tight five just turned into a tight fifteen. I'm way too late getting back."

"I'll pick you up at Nora's house? Maybe before your rehearsal this time next week? Four?"

"I can meet you," she volunteered. "I don't want you to have to rush over from work. Besides, I like the excuse to drive out and see how the town has changed."

"Alright," Ellis agreed. "Warm and Plenty sound good? It's still got great blueberry bagels."

"Sounds perfect," she breathed, feeling that familiar

flutter in her chest.

He squeezed her hand. "See you then."

They parted ways, him back to his law firm and her back to rehearsal. Alone in the cold evening, Lizzie was suddenly aware of exactly how late she was getting back to the theater.

Had she forgotten how dynamic he was? Or just tried to suppress it? Once more, she reflected on how the longer she was in Warner Robins, the more the line between actual memory and her own opinions were blurred. Ten years was a long time. A very long time. Something gnawed at the back of her brain.

"Shoot," she muttered to herself and took off at a run. She sent out a silent prayer that no one else from high school would have to witness her out of breath, hobbling, half-soaked in men's sweatpants and a hole-riddled high school football t-shirt. She picked up the pace, just in case.

Lizzie slipped back into rehearsal through the back door of the Baron. The slow, soft lyrics of "Anatevka" rang out, reverberating through the space. They'd already gotten around to learning the closing number without her. Shoot.

Her stomach twisted as she joined in the number at the back of the group, taking special care to keep her sheet music quiet as she opened it up. She hated being late. It was unprofessional and just lazy. She'd gotten away with it this time, but she couldn't make skipping out a habit in the future. Even for cute ex-boyfriends.

"*Ellis?*" Grace mouthed at her behind her sheet music. Lizzie blushed and nodded, to which Grace gave an impressed smile and motioned for her to weave her way through the cast toward their friend group.

Even barely rehearsed, the music was beautiful. Lizzie had always loved this song. *Fiddler on the Roof* was one of the first musicals she could remember from her youth. She'd rented out an old VHS copy from the local library and spent hours watching in front of the TV while her dad slowly got stoned in the armchair behind her. "Anatevka" was a goodbye song, sung by Jewish villagers who had to part with their home if they wanted to survive. It was a feeling she could understand well.

Lizzie was regretting her overstay at the coffee shop. She really should have been at rehearsal, should have been more responsible. It was no wonder—

"Cut!" David Flannery's voice, strong and firm, cut through the last piano note. Had the last hour of rehearsal flown by already? Lizzie had been so lost in the music that she'd barely noticed.

David was standing on a crate on the floor just off the stage, the sleeves of the day's navy Mr. Rogers cardigan rolled up once more to better allow him to direct the music. "Great first attempt, people. You made it through a lot of music today. Give yourselves a round of applause."

The group lit up, cheering and hollering in equal parts excitement and exhaustion.

David help up a hand. "We'll call it a day for now. I'll see you all on Wednesday for the next rehearsal."

Still buzzing, the cast members began to put away their music and shuffle off the stage.

"How about Tequila's tonight, y'all?" Ashley asked, slipping her music into a black bag.

"Ugh, I wish," moaned Grace. "Boyd's got inventory, so I need to head home and relieve the sitter."

"I'll pass, too, love," Clint said, leaning forward to kiss Ashley goodbye on the cheek. "Teddy has Chicken Marsala at home and he will kill me if I miss out on another Hello Fresh meal."

"Lizzie?" Ashley asked.

"Hmm?" She'd been distracted watching the other cast members file out. Cliques like hers had formed already, friends walking out arm in arm, laughing. Other individuals lingered, testing out bars of music they hadn't felt were quite right.

At the front of the stage, Margo packed up her sheet music and said goodbye to David. Lizzie watched as one of the dashing young men from the chorus approached the accompanist with what could only be a truly horrific pickup line. Margo was as gracious as ever, laughing at the guy's line but waving him off. Lizzie couldn't help herself—she took note of how Margo's eyes darted to David, clearly asking him to step in without having to voice a single word. Lizzie watched as David stepped between the two of them, a hand on Margo's forearm as he rebuffed the particularly forward suitor.

"Tequila's?" Ashley asked again. "Wanna go?"

"Sorry," Lizzie apologized. Her attentions jerked back to her group. "Fullmer and Hazel are probably driving Nora and Bill up the wall. I'd better give them advance notice before I bail for a whole evening."

"Suit yourself," Ashley sighed. "But if I pick up an addiction from drinking alone, it will be on all of y'all's consciences." They all laughed and started to head for the door.

"Lizzie? A word?"

Lizzie stopped short at the sound of David's voice, her stomach immediately clenching into a tight ball. He stood alone at the edge of the stage with his things packed, the lingering cast members all beginning to file out around him. Lizzie could already feel the lump forming in her throat as she waved her friends off and headed back to speak with him.

"Are you happy to be in the show?" he asked, crossing his arms as he studied her face.

"Oh," Lizzie let out a half-laugh, relieved to be asked such a simple question. "God, of course I am. I've always loved *Fiddler*."

"Then maybe you should take it more seriously." David's eyes were unforgiving and cold. "You were the last one to show up from break. I expect more from my leading actors."

"I'm sorry, David," she started. "Something came up and time got away from me. It won't happen again."

"You're right," he said. "It won't. I'm sure you remember that we had a lot of auditioners who wanted your part. If you're not going to take rehearsal seriously, then I can call any one of them."

"I'm sorry," Lizzie's voice was coming out more defensive than she intended it to. "I really will stay on top of things from now on."

"Be sure you do."

"... Is that all?"

David nodded. Lizzie swung her bag back over her shoulder and turned to head for the door. She was surprised when she heard his voice call out again, quieter this time, no longer the firm, commanding tones of his directing. "I'm... glad you're back."

She turned back to see him. He was a different man than the one she'd left behind after graduation. He was confident, strong, and he knew how to take care of himself. But for the first time since she'd come home to the theater, she saw the David Flannery she remembered from high school. Open. Vulnerable.

"I think I am, too."

CHAPTER 9

*D*espite her best efforts, there seemed to be no way to make rehearsal clothes look any sexier than the t-shirt and sweatpants that Ellis had seen Lizzie in last.

She had tried on countless yoga pants and oversized sweaters, all of which made her feel too young and silly. Like she was trying to recapture high school. She certainly didn't want Ellis to get *that* impression. Gym shorts made her look boxy and lazy. An over-eager and romance-crazed Hazel had sat on Lizzie's bed next to Nora, helping her mom to prep for the big coffee date and happily suggesting a vibrant pair of fluffy pink legwarmers that she had found stashed in a costume box at the bottom of the closet. Sorry, kid. Those definitely weren't going to do the trick either.

In the end, Lizzie had settled on a simple workout top and running leggings. Anything else felt too much like a lie. And she already felt like she was lying to her friends enough just by returning to her hometown.

Nevertheless, she set back her shoulders and smiled broadly on her way out the door. With Hazel firmly on the hook and invested in her mother's dating success, it only seemed right to feign complete confidence. No need to plant her own self-doubt and criticisms into her daughter's already boy-crazed, male-validation-seeking mind. Besides, maybe if she faked it enough she'd start to believe it.

Lizzie entered the Warm and Plenty coffee shop with caution. The panic was back in full force and elevated from its usual status as she had neither friends nor children to serve as a buffer to her interaction with a familiar face.

Ellis saw her immediately, flagging her down from his spot by a window. He, of course, looked very well put-together. He still wore the sharp, crisp suit from his workday, and his tie was ever so slightly undone, as though he'd just begun to relax. It was a far cry from his football uniform back in high school, but it was a look that very much suited him, nonetheless.

"I think I overdid it," he said, smiling as he took Lizzie's arm to lead them back to a booth he had procured. "I knew you were running on limited time and so I ordered one of, well, almost *everything*."

Sure enough, there were coffee cups strewn about the table, each venting a satisfying puff of steam. Lizzie's stomach gurgled out loud. "This is amazing! I'm absolutely starving." She snatched a cup marked "mocha" and took a gulp. Thank goodness for a drink to mask her face.

She turned to Ellis, grinning. Much to her surprise, his face was its own shade of pink. The evidence of his nerves began to dissipate as he realized that he had pleased her.

Was it really possible that she had made Ellis Clarke feel nervous? Lizzie couldn't help but feel a little pleased. He had always seemed so unattainable, even when she was dating him. It was oddly flattering to know that, in this one moment, she was the one who had the power.

They sat down and Ellis selected his own drink: black coffee, double shot of espresso.

"I won't lie," he started. "I was definitely crossing my fingers that you wouldn't take this drink. I would seem a lot less manly and impressive if I was left with my second favorite coffee, the chai latte."

She laughed. "I don't think that's possible."

Ellis sat back in his chair, folding his arms to size her up. "So tell me everything. I hate that I missed a decade of the most interesting girl in the world."

"Oh God, there's nothing to tell." She shook her head.

Lizzie could feel that creeping sense of unease again, the one she got whenever the subject of her embarrassing last decade was broached. He'd called her "the most interesting girl in the world." That was going to sound super ironic when she launched into a description of serving drunk trunk drivers and pinching pennies instead of starring on Broadway.

Still ... she couldn't help but feel like this was the opportunity to ease him into her life. She couldn't hold on to her shameful truth for forever. Maybe a handsome face from the past who genuinely wanted good things for Lizzie could help her to reconcile who she once was with who she had become. And more importantly—with a little bit of luck and a few more of these charming coffee shop dates—maybe Ellis could become a vital part in her future.

"Honestly, I didn't get to do any of the stuff I set out to do." She started to hesitantly explain, eyes stubbornly trained on her mocha. "I've spent the past ten years working at a crap diner out in New Jersey, barely making ends meet. I just... couldn't hack it in the big city."

Once the words were spoken, she couldn't take them back. Lizzie dreaded looking up, but finally she willed herself to do so. Ellis had a thoughtful look on his face as he reached across the table to squeeze her hand, sending little sparks shooting through her fingertips.

"Lizzie, at least you went for it." He said. "That's more than almost anyone in Warner Robins can say. Even I'm still living five minutes away from my dad and shopping at the same grocery store. You put yourself out there. That's amazing."

She felt a burning in her chest. She squeezed his hand back, trying not to let a stupid happy grin overtake her face.

"So what else?" he asked. "Any other men I need to watch out for?"

Lizzie's mind flashed to two familiar faces. Fullmer, her small, scrupulous son. And with him came Hazel, her wild-child daughter.

The words caught in her mouth. She might not be ready to talk about that part of her life quite yet. Her children weren't secret, but they were sacred. She had to get the timing just right.

"No, definitely no men." Lizzie smiled and shook her head. "I don't think I've been on a date this planned out and formal in at least five years."

"Come on!" Ellis smacked a hand to his chest in dramatic astonishment. "Now the standards for this date are impossibly high. I should have ordered you one of all the pastries, too."

They both laughed again, and Lizzie could feel the tension of talking about her private life slip away. It was easy with Ellis. Familiar. She could get used to it.

She lost herself in the talking. She really had forgotten just how charming he was. He supplied her with funny anecdotes about the lackluster paralegals at his law firm and made her tear up filling her in on his mother's death a few years back. He talked and she listened and the coffee just kept coming and coming until she was losing herself in altogether too much cream and sugar.

After what felt like forever, her alarm beeped, signaling the need to jet off for rehearsal.

"Ugh," she moaned. "I hate that I have to go."

"I'm not letting you leave without plans for another outing," Ellis announced. "Cubano's. Friday night. Do you have rehearsal?"

"No." Lizzie smiled. Her heart was already picking up the pace in anticipation of a date still days away. "I can meet you there at six?"

"That sounds like absolute perfection," Ellis said.

CHAPTER 10

*L*izzie's elementary school was the first building in Warner Robins that fit perfectly into the way she had remembered it. The walls, gray cinderblock with bright, happy murals of children recycling and gardening, had aged and chipped in the years since she'd been away, but remained the vibrant, cheery welcome she could remember from a thousand days entering Russell Elementary. The building even smelled the same, like cafeteria food and wood chips and ancient carpet that probably ought to have been replaced back when Lizzie was a student there. It was all perfect.

Lizzie and the Grant-Thornton clan had arrived in their Sunday best for the kids' fall musical: *Jack and the Beanstalk.* They shuffled into a row of metal folding chairs, the crowd around them buzzing with parental excitement.

"Jeez, you'd think this was the Tony awards," Lizzie muttered.

"Is it not?" Nora asked, wide-eyed. "Mary-Kate is going to be so disappointed."

"Because playing Jack's cow clearly requires the performance of a lifetime." Poppy smiled. "I have never seen that child so thrilled."

Bill balanced young Caroline on his lap, who was engrossed in the carefully folded paper program. "She might have a professional rival in Townsperson Number One," he winked at Lizzie. "I think I've heard Hazel singing in her sleep. Looks like she got a gene or two from her mama."

Lizzie blushed, but she couldn't help but smile with pride. "We're just lucky we arrived in town with time for the kids to get cast. Speaking of which, does anyone know what Fullmer is doing?"

"That's a surprise," Poppy said, who mimed zipping his lips and throwing away the key.

"Don't be creepy, old man, you're not allowed to conspire with my kid." Lizzie elbowed him and Poppy grinned. He put a finger to his lips as the cafeteria lights began to fade.

The musical began with a rush of young bodies running across the stage bearing ribbons on sticks, miming out the magical forces that would later turn Jack's beans into a towering stalk. Mary-Kate was the first of their kids to make her appearance, her jack-o-lantern smile painted white and black. She mooed earlier than her first cue and looked a little embarrassed, but made up for the gaffe with an extra-loud moo at her on-stage death that got a rumbling laugh from the parents in the audience. Lizzie saw Bill take Nora's hand and squeeze it with pride.

It wasn't hard to pick out Hazel in the crowd of towns-people. She was the only kid not trying to make eyes at her mom or wave at a friend in the audience. Instead, she was completely plugged into the acting, staring intently up at the beanstalk as Jack climbed and yelling, "Be careful, young lad!" at just the right moment. Lizzie felt her own surge of delight. Someone squeezed her hand, just as she'd seen Bill do with Nora. She looked up to see Poppy smiling his crooked little smile once more at her in the soft cafeteria light.

She leaned over to him. "I still haven't seen Fullmer."

"Wait for it," he whispered, nodding toward the stage.

Jack was up in the clouds now, taking in the forbidden wonders of the giant's castle. A first grade boy posed, stoic and serious, as the goose who laid golden eggs. Jack retrieved him with care and started back for the paper mâché beanstalk when—FE FI FO FUM—the giant (an extra-tall sixth grader standing on a box behind the curtains) peeked his head out of his castle. Jack fell back in surprise, his tumble punctuated with a silly tune from a trio of horns.

"*Fullmer?*"

Lizzie leaned forward in awe as Poppy crossed his arms and smiled in satisfaction for his great surprise. "Kid's been trying out the sax in my garage while you've been out running errands or at rehearsal. He's got a knack for it."

Fullmer stood just under the stage, looking like a beatnik in a smart black turtleneck and cocked newsboy's cap. The saxophone he carried looked at least half his size, but he held it up and blew it with pride. He picked out each note with precision, holding his own with the two sweating and nervous trio members playing at his sides. Fullmer's grin was the biggest of all the students' Lizzie had seen that night. The edges of his smile shown through even when he blew into the instrument, unable to be contained.

"But he's never had a lesson before," she whispered to Poppy. "It's not like we could afford them."

Poppy shrugged, still grinning up at his working pupil.

"Turns out that years of obsessive theoretical study can get you pretty far."

"So you're telling me that *The Music Man* was accurate?" Lizzie raised an eyebrow.

Poppy shushed her with that finger to his mouth again. "Child, just sit back and enjoy the genius."

Lizzie laughed at loud as she saw Fullmer counting under his breath. The old obsessive habit was of some good use here, serving as a means to help him find the beat. She was transfixed on his playing from then on, sitting on the edge of her seat as he focused on finding each carefully rehearsed note. When the play ended and her saxophone player and Townsperson Number One took the stage once more for their final curtain call, she stood up, hooting and hollering like all the other excited parents around her. Her face could hardly contain her massive grin.

"John Coltrane and Judy Garland, defying time and space to appear in a special one-night only performance!" She rushed the kids as they arrived at their row in the cafeteria, scooping them up into a suffocating three-way hug.

"Mo-om, Drew Harper will see!" Hazel chastised her, but Lizzie could still hear a note of pride in her voice.

Nearby, Bill, Poppy, and Nora took turns giving Mary-Kate her own hugs. Lizzie watched as Nora pulled her close to her breast, holding her for far longer than the others had. She stroked her dark hair and planted a tender kiss on the top of her head, closing her eyes to breathe in her scent. To memorize the moment.

"Well, that was really something," Nora pronounced, pulling away and looking more than a little misty-eyed. "I think we need to celebrate that performance. How about ... Pizza Parade?"

At once, all of the children exploded into an excited

uproar. "Yes, Mom, *please* can we go?" begged Hazel, pulling at her mother's shirt.

Even Fullmer was taken in. "They have Skee-ball there," he noted with wide, wondrous eyes.

"I'll pass tonight," Bill chimed in, leaning over to kiss his wife on the cheek as he scooped up young Caroline. "It's somebody's bedtime soon."

"*Nooo!*" Caroline began to wail and her tears sprung forth, rolling rivers down her little brown cheeks.

"I'm out, too," Poppy said, slapping a hand on Bill's shoulder and offering to take the crying Caroline into his own arms. "Old man's gotta get his beauty rest."

"Whatever, losers." Nora winked and turned back to the kids. "Minivan's in the front lot. Last one in is a rotten egg."

The adults left the cafeteria together, watching the kids giggle and push each other out of the way to race to the car. Nora took Lizzie's hand in her own as they made their way out.

"Pizza Parade serves beer, just so you know," she whispered.

"Cigarettes *and* alcohol? You are full of vices these days, Dr. Grant!"

"Just trying to live a little." Nora grinned.

Pizza Parade was packed with other parents celebrating the big elementary school musical, but Nora and Lizzie hardly noticed. The night kicked up into a wild frenzy, full of the kids stacking up mountains of yellow paper tickets on their empty plates, harried young waiters running back and forth between demanding tables, and sweating pitchers of beer that never seemed to stay full between the two old friends. The girls talked for hours, fully relaxing as they laughed and reminisced about their own school days.

"Good night, nurse; have you seen the time?" The world

outside of the neon-sprayed Pizza Parade windows had gone completely dark. Nora looked at her watch, mild worry playing out on swimming, drunken eyes. She tried to stand up but stumbled into Lizzie, who caught her before she fell.

"Careful, you'll get yourself covered in grease and old soda."

"Ack!" Nora laughed, the sound a little too loud. "Oh Lord, I'm drunk."

"Ya think?" Lizzie giggled, too. She stood up and put an arm out for her friend. "I'll drive. Let's grab the kids."

The pair of them flagged down the children, who ran over with arms full of arcade prizes and nary a complaint. The house was close and, despite the persistent buzz she felt at the back of her head, Lizzie was able to navigate the familiar Warner Robins back roads with ease. They pulled into the driveway and the kids scrambled over one another to get inside and compare winnings. Lizzie popped the keys and sunk back into her chair, one hand over her tired eyes.

"We're too old for this," she laughed.

"Speak for yourself!" Nora was curled up like a cat in her captain's chair, her head resting against the window.

Lizzie folded her arms and closed her eyes. "It's official. Nora Grant, you have out-partied the party queen. High school me would be proud."

Nora laughed, the sound coming out quiet this time. "Everything is perfect," she mumbled from her ball in the chair. "You're back in town, Poppy's retired, Bill's work is finally going to start slowing down ... I'm not going to miss out on a second of it."

"Are you sure you're going to remember any of it if you're wasted?" Lizzie thumped Nora on the back of the head. Her friend sat up, a lazy half-smile on her happy face.

"I'm just trying it all," she answered. "I'm trying every last, beautiful thing out there."

A knock sounded on the car window and Lizzie turned to see the kids pressing their little faces up against the glass.

"Mo-om," Hazel said as the window rolled down. "We tried knocking but no one let us in."

Nora smacked her forehead. "They must be asleep. I've got a key."

They left the minivan parked out front and made their way to the back deck as a group. With a flourish, Nora produced a small red University of Georgia key from her handbag and unlocked the door. The kids piled through, running in a stampede for the stairs.

"Don't you dare wake up baby Caroline!" Lizzie whispered after them as loud as she dared.

Nora giggled. "Oh, boy. I'm never going to make it up the stairs in this state."

"I've got you." Lizzie came to her rescue with an extended arm.

"Wait!" Nora stopped in the doorway and pulled out her handbag once more. She fished around in it for a moment, handing her wallet, a pack of tissues, and a thin tube of lipstick to Lizzie. Finally, she found what she was looking for.

"Here," she told Lizzie. "You should have this back."

Nora dropped something in her palm. Lizzie opened her hand. Inside lay a small green and pink key, identical in every way but the design to the first key they had used. The casing had rubbed away around the edges, revealing beaten, dull brass.

"I haven't seen this in..."

"Ten years?" Nora was smiling at her in the darkness.

"I'm drunk, but I can still do basic math. I'm a doc-*tor* after all."

"Ten years," Lizzie agreed, laughing. "I'm surprised you kept my spare."

"It wasn't mine to throw away," Nora replied, shrugging and shutting the back door behind them. "Now you can come and go as you please."

"I'm sure Poppy will be glad that I won't have to resort to breaking in through the windows like I used to before you gave me the key."

"Poppy's just glad to have you home. We all are." Nora reached out and took her friend's hand. They walked together through the dark of the first floor and over to the stairs.

"Home." Lizzie tested the word on her tongue. Nora squeezed her hand before they headed upstairs and off to bed.

CHAPTER 11

"Lizzie!" Ellis had a corner booth at Cubano's, where he stood waving her over.

She found herself blushing already. At Nora's behest, Lizzie had borrowed a brilliant red dress and put on eyeshadow for the first time in what felt like years. It had taken her over an hour to get ready for the evening, which was a little embarrassing for her. Standing in the door of the restaurant, she felt like she was play-acting, pretending to be someone young and beautiful and carefree that she clearly was not. In heels that were just a touch too tall for her, she stumbled her way back to the booth where Ellis stood waiting.

He, of course, was a knock-out. He wore a dark suit and a gray shirt and a striped tie—an actual, manly tie—as though Lizzie was an event to prepare for of the most sacred kind. He ran a hand through his thick blonde hair before offering to help her slide into the booth across from his own seat.

Lizzie could feel him taking her in—every inch of bright red dress and carefully applied makeup. Ellis' desire for her couldn't be missed. He made no move to hide himself, to shrink away. Suddenly she found herself feeling even more exposed and nervous than when she had entered. She was grateful when he sat down, grinning at her with flashing white teeth.

"I'm so glad we could both make it. For a while there, I didn't think my secretary would let me duck out early from some extra projects I'd taken on."

"Sounds like you work hard," Lizzie said.

"I've just got a goal and I want to make it happen. And soon!" He smiled again. "You should see the ranch style I've got my eye on near Main Street. Pool in the backyard, new kitchen, it's perfect. I'm so close to making an offer."

A pool in the backyard. Lizzie forgot all about the exposed feeling from a moment ago as she thought once more of the kind of life that Ellis Clarke had to offer. He was handsome. Accomplished. Stable. Part of her wanted to reach out and take his hand now.

"Would it make you uncomfortable if I told you I've been looking forward to this all week?" Ellis asked her with a little laugh.

Lizzie blushed again. "I have, too."

Ellis leaned back in his seat, still smiling at her. "God, it's still surreal that you're back. I never thought I'd see you again after you disappeared post-graduation. I forgot to mention that I wrote to you, ya know."

He hadn't. Lizzie knew that for sure. She'd had her mail forwarded before she left for the city, not wanting to have to deal with her father or any of his girlfriends ever again. Still, she could forgive him for the lie. It flattered her, even. Ellis was trying to impress her. He was trying to win her over.

"Oh? You did?" She replied. "I never got much of anything out in the city. Unreliable mailman, I guess."

"Yeah, that must be it. So tell me all about New York City." His eyes shown big and bright. "There are a million questions I wanted to ask you last time, but not enough minutes in the day. Are you sure you weren't in any shows I might have seen? I make a trip every summer out to see the cousins, and I find it hard to believe that you weren't cast in anything with a talent like yours."

"I'm sure I wasn't," she said, clipping the thread of conversation short. "But what about you? You're at your dad's firm?"

"Hardly," Ellis laughed. "He was always too small time, too country. After law school, I got in good with some big wigs out in Macon. They run central Georgia. Dad can keep his firm. It's not like he would have ever made me a partner, anyway. He spent my teenage years reminding me that I was a freeloader."

Ellis' eyes clouded over, the first frown Lizzie had seen from him yet, tugging down the corners of his broad mouth. She remembered his father, so the opposite of her own. With the exception of a thick, dark head of hair that was graying at the temples at 45, he would be the spitting image of everything his son was now right down to the expensive suit and tie. He was calloused, though, hardened beyond what one usually finds in a small-town lawyer. Grayson Clarke ran Warner Robins and he knew it.

"Sounds like it might be time for drinks?" Lizzie suggested.

Ellis brightened back up. "Aleja?" He waved over a perky brunette waitress, who beamed when she saw him. She bounced over to their table, putting a hand on Ellis' shoulder and smiling.

"Mr. Clarke! It's a pleasure to have you back in."

"Can we have two Margaritas and a coffee, please?" The

waitress tucked her pad into her apron, not needing to jot anything down, and started to step away. Lizzie couldn't help but wonder if the order was familiar to her. An unexpected pang of jealousy needled at her chest.

"Can I actually just get a glass of wine?" Lizzie piped up. "Sorry," she apologized to Ellis. "I have to get up for an early rehearsal tomorrow."

Ellis reached out to the waitress, stopping her with a slight wave of his hand. "So sorry, Aleja, wine for the lady, please. But still send that second Margarita. If I can't convince her to drink it, maybe we'll send it your way."

The waitress giggled and waved him off. "Sure thing, Mr. Clarke."

He turned back to Lizzie, taking her hand in his once more. His fingers sent a tingle through her palm as he stroked her skin with a familiar, easy touch. "More rehearsal in the morning, huh? That Flannery takes everything so seriously. What show are you doing?"

"*Fiddler on the Roof.* I'm Golde again, just like in high school."

"That's amazing! I can't wait to see it." He crossed his arms, leaning back in his side of the booth to smile at her. "I'll admit, we gave up our season tickets to the Baron ages ago. They're always a little too predictable, never casting anything exciting or producing anything edgy. You really ought to perform at the Fox, you know. You're so talented. Just saw *Book of Mormon* there last year."

"I don't know," she demurred, shaking her head. "The Fox mostly does regional productions. I'd have to go to a huge cattle call for auditions and then I'd probably be required to tour, which means—"

Lizzie had almost launched into talking about her kids. Why did she stop short? Her own hesitancy surprised her as she realized that she still hadn't told Ellis about Hazel and Fullmer.

For the entirety of their short lives, Lizzie had kept her twins safely guarded, protected from the hazards of an unpredictable world. Maybe this closeness was partially responsible for Hazel's attachment to all things male or the middle-aged man aesthetic that Fullmer had naturally acquired: they were both figuring out how to cope without a father in the house, and Lizzie had limited their outlets outside of the home to sort out such complex emotions. The truth was, she was scared to open them up to new faces and new places. Dating men, returning to Warner Robins... It all still felt like a major risk.

Lizzie's thoughts were interrupted as Aleja the Waitress returned with their drinks, her perky breasts almost spilling out of her low-cut t-shirt as she reached across the table to place down the water. Lizzie's hand drifted on instinct to her own stomach, floating its way up to the bottom of her bra to finger its ragged lace through her dress.

She could picture her body, a stark contrast to this young girl's. Before she had come out that night, she had stood in front of Nora's bedroom mirror, pale and naked, holding the red dress in her hesitant hands. Once more, Lizzie found herself reflecting on how much she had changed from the girl who left Warner Robins a decade prior. Her skin hung loose around her waist and thighs, highlighted by thick, white tiger stripes, the product of a sixty-pound weight gain during twin pregnancy. She was skinny, but untoned, her belly button sinking in as though it were trying to disappear into her body. Her breasts hung heavy and round, extending into small pink nipples that looked—for desperate want of a much better adjective —*used*.

Lizzie had heard other women describe their post-pregnancy bodies as something of which to be proud. Their stretch marks were battle wounds, badges of honor that reflected a time-honored tradition of carrying on a family's legacy. Lizzie's battle wounds marked a war that she had lost. Her children weren't a part of any family's legacy. They were fatherless, near motherless with how much Lizzie had to slave to provide for them, and the marks that they had left on her skin were a reminder of her deep shame.

Telling Ellis about her children now felt ... well, she didn't know if she felt ready for that. Even more dangerous than the inherent risk in exposing her children to the rest of the world was the risk in Lizzie owning up to every choice and transition that she had made for over a decade. To acknowledge the kids' existence out loud was to acknowledge that she was a far cry from the girlfriend he'd had back in high school. She had changed. Irrevocably.

"For someone so talented, you have so many excuses for not doing the things that make you happy." Ellis reached across the table and ran his thumb across her cheekbone as he brought her back to their original line of conversation. "Well theater or no theater, I'm glad that you agreed to come out with me tonight. There's so much I want to rediscover about you." Lizzie felt a shiver as his thumb left her cheek to glide across her bottom lip.

"Can I take your order?" The waitress had returned from checking in with another table and now waited—smile plastered on and eyes glued on Ellis' lingering hand—to help them.

"I'm so sorry," Lizzie apologized. "I haven't had a moment to look at the menu."

"No pressure, Lizzie, but I think you'd love the Arroz con

Pollo," Ellis said with a knowing smile. "Trust me. Two of those, please, Aleja."

"Sure thing." She was off to the kitchen and Lizzie breathed a sigh of relief at her exit.

"So," Ellis took hold once more of the conversation. "Tell me everything that I've missed. Give me the Lizzie Hancock play-by-play."

Lizzie took a deep gulp of her wine. "Oh, jeez. I'm embarrassed to give you too much information on my sad decade."

"Oh, please," He waved her off. "Let's call it a Two Minute Brag. You can give me the highlight reel so you don't leave a date with me feeling bad."

"The Two Minute Brag?" She repeated, eyebrow raised. "That's cute. Is that a gimmick you pull out on all your dates?"

It was Ellis' turn to blush. "You can read right through my playbook, huh?"

"We dated for a long time." She smiled. "I think I still know a thing or two about you."

"Ok," he admitted. "So I pull out the gimmick with the girls that I like. But to be fair, you're the first girl that's really held my interest in a very long time."

Lizzie felt him reach under the table to squeeze her knee. Much to her surprise, his fingers brushed a trail up her thigh. She hadn't expected such physicality so soon. But as much as she was attracted to Ellis, instinct made her put a hand under the table to meet his fingers at the hem of her dress. Lizard brain or just years of habit? Whatever it was, she smiled past the feeling, feeling a little hot under the collar.

"Well, if it's a tired gimmick, maybe I can refresh it with my very non-Middle Georgia brag sheet." She said, taking back control of the conversation. "I'm sure all the debutants and pageant queens give you the same nonsense every time about saving kittens and organizing food banks, right?"

"Don't forget curing malaria and accomplishing world peace." He smiled.

"Hmm ..." Lizzie thought for a moment. Her truth definitely wouldn't sound anything like that. "Well, I was on my own for a long time after high school. I paid my own way for everything. Got a job. My own apartment. Bet a lot of your trust fund babies can't say that, right?"

"I like a woman who can take care of herself," he said.

"That's me, for sure. I make a mean omelet. Taught myself that, too. I can keep a weekly grocery bill under a hundred dollars—"

"Impressive. I buy that amount in takeout lunches every week. Sounds like I might need a private tutoring session."

"Thank you, thank you. And—" her voice caught in her throat for a moment. *Do it. Do it now.* "—I'm a mom. To two amazing kids. Twins."

No quick, witty reply came. Lizzie's stomach wrenched inside of her.

"Well," she said, her voice coming out awkward and halting. The panic was rising in her throat once more, and every section of her insides were pulling her in the direction of the Cubano's exit. "It's been a lovely date. Thank you, Ellis—"

She started to stand, but he put a hand on her arm. "You have two kids," he smiled. "That's amazing. Amazing! I bet you're an incredible mom."

Her stomach continued to twist, her worry clouding over his kind words. "C'mon," he urged her, pulling her down into the booth right next to him to put an arm around her shoulders. "So, you've got kids. Did you think I was going to run for the hills?"

"In my experience, most men do."

"If there's one thing I pride myself on, it's that I am *not* most men." Ellis pulled her closer and tucked a loose strand of hair behind her ear. Lizzie felt the tingle once more, his touch branding into her neck.

"No," she breathed. "You are not."

"You can't run from me, Lizzie Hancock. Not again." The waitress interrupted their moment to bring two heaping dishes of chicken and rice.

"Oh, God," Lizzie groaned. "That smells amazing."

"It tastes even better." Ellis pulled over a bowl of bread and pushed her plate in front of her. "Try it with the margarita, Liz. Flannery won't be the wiser tomorrow at rehearsal."

"I don't know ..."

"Besides," he started. "A mom of twins definitely needs some loosening up now and then."

"Alright," she relented and grabbed a salted glass. "Wow, that's sweet."

"But good, right?"

"You were right." She smiled and took another sip.

"So, how old are they?" Ellis took a big bite of his chicken. "Your kids, I mean."

Lizzie pulled the margarita toward her once more, hoping to bury her face behind it. "... Nine."

Even through her massive gulp, she could see him doing the mental math.

"Wow, you must have had them—"

"Yeah," she nodded. "Met a guy right after graduation. Thought he was 'the one,' you know? Turns out he was just 'the one who couldn't be bothered with a condom.'"

Ellis laughed. "His loss," he said, taking another bite. He moaned and closed his eyes. "Ugh, this is divine. Mine must be better than yours. Why don't you sound like you're in the throes of ecstasy?"

She giggled. He reached over, spooning up a bite from her plate, and offered it to her. "Try it."

She leaned forward and let him feed her. "Wow." Even with her eyes closed as she enjoyed the bite, she could feel Ellis' intense gaze on her face.

"I think," he started. "This would be even better on a tostada." He pulled the bread bowl closer. "One, two, three, four..."

"You're counting the bread?" She asked.

"I think they stiffed us. Hey! Sweetheart!" He snapped his fingers in the air and Aleja the Waitress came trotting over, eager to please once more. "Do you think we could get some more tostadas? Usually there are six in a bowl."

"Of course," she answered, smiling. Lizzie felt a surge in her chest as Aleja took in the sight of Ellis, arm draped casually across her thigh.

"You're going to love it," He smiled as the waitress left. "You don't know what you've been missing all these years you've been away from our fair city! The food! The culture! We're going places, baby."

"I'm starting to get an idea," she smiled.

CHAPTER 12

*L*izzie couldn't remember the last time she felt so tired. But she also couldn't remember the last time she felt so proud of herself.

Rehearsals had gotten intense, with the hours stretching out longer and later as opening night drew closer. Lizzie spent her days taking care of the house errands, schlepping the kids from dance to soccer, and helping them hit their homework before packing her black duffel to head off to evening rehearsal. The process had grown to be familiar, comforting, and also completely exhausting.

She loved every minute of it.

"Let's run it again, people! Margo, give them an eight count in." David's latest get-up was a navy and burgundy striped cardigan over his usual black turtleneck. Once more, he had the sleeves pushed up to his elbows as he worked at the front of the stage, waving his arms in enthusiastic, comical motions as he directed his ensemble through the fast-paced number "To Life."

"Alright, cut! Cut!" David waved at Margo to stop the piano. "Ashley! I know you're a ballerina. I've seen your resume, and I saw you in *Cats* last year. But can you give me a little more street dancer and a little less *Nutcracker*? I'm not buying it."

Ashley, donned in a heavy coat and boots to play one of the bar patrons dancing in the ensemble, nodded, but looked a little worse for wear.

"You got this," Lizzie whispered.

Ashley nodded again, biting her lip. "This is the second time he's called me out."

"Let's go again. From the top of the chorus, Margo." David clapped his hands. "Five, six, seven, eight!"

The group started back into the wild chaos of the drunken bar scene, bodies flying into raucous flips and jumps. It was at least the tenth time the group had run the number that night, but Lizzie still felt the smile pulling on her lips as the fun of the pandemonium overtook her. She didn't know that she would ever get sick of dancing "To Life."

"Cut!" David called out, rubbing a frustrated hand on his forehead. "Ashley ..."

Ashley burst into tears, collapsing into Lizzie's side and covering her bright red cheeks with her hands. David booked it over. Worry lines of a new sort creased his face.

"Whoa, wait a minute." He pulled Ashley over to him, who let her weight fall onto his chest as she started to sob. David waved his arms at the rest of the group. "Take five, guys."

Lizzie rubbed Ashley's back. "It's ok, Ash."

"You're tired," David said. "I've been running you too hard this week."

"No," Ashley moaned into his shirt. "I'm just the idiot who can't nail the backflip."

"You nail it every time!" David laughed and pushed

Ashley back with two hands on her shoulders, his worried eyes searching her face. "It's just that you're Misty Freaking Copeland out there. So graceful. You're the best dancer I have, no doubt about it."

"David, you can't tell me that I need work *and* that I'm your best dancer." Ashley laughed a little, rubbing the tears from her eyes with the sleeve of her sweater.

"Yes, I very well can. All I meant was that you might want to rough it up a little. Dance like one of us lumbering men if you're going to be playing one." Ashley rolled her eyes and David turned to Lizzie. "Back me up here."

Lizzie was taken aback by the invitation to join in. "He's right," she assured her friend. "Somehow you look *too* beautiful when you dance. I hate you."

Ashley laughed, the tears starting to fade away. "Come on."

"If you don't make any changes at all, I'll still be getting the best dancing from you that I'm getting from anyone in this cast," David said. "I'm only pushing you because I know you can do even better."

"He's right," Lizzie agreed.

Ashley sighed. "Well, I really wish I hadn't lost it in front of the group just now. I'm never going to live that down."

"Are you kidding?" David laughed. It was a deep, happy sound that resonated out from his chest. "Don't you remember when I broke my ankle during *Rocky Horror* a few years back? A full face of Frank N. Furter makeup ruined by my man tears. If I can come back from that, you can come back from this."

"Don't think that any of us have forgotten that." Ashley winked and David playfully pushed her shoulder. The cast was starting to shuffle back onto the stage. "Can I just go take a minute to clean off my face?"

"Take all the time you need." Ashley left and Lizzie started to head back for her place in the number. David grabbed her arm, pulling her back. "Can you go follow her and make sure she's alright? Grab her a Coke and I'll pay you back."

His hand lingered for a moment on her elbow as his worried eyes followed Ashley out the stage door. "Don't worry about it," Lizzie answered. David looked back down at her and she saw it again: that glimpse of the teenage boy she'd left behind in Warner Robins. He was looking to her for help, for advice. She got the sense that he was taking her in, all of her at once. Really looking at her for the first time since they had been re-introduced to one another. Lizzie felt a tightening in her chest. For a moment, he had forgotten all that had happened between them.

David pulled back his hand and crossed his arms, realizing that he had lingered for a moment too long. "Thanks," he said, his voice curt. "Take your own five."

He turned to head back to rehearsal and Lizzie started to follow Ashley's path out through the stage door. When David had pulled his arm away, she had gotten a good look at his tattoo sleeves. They were the biggest change since graduation, even over his weight loss and the thick brown beard. She'd spotted his mother's name, Trish, running near his wrist. There was a landscape, too. It had looked a bit like the familiar forests that ran all throughout Warner Robins. Kudzu, heavy and dominant even in ink, climbed from his right wrist up to his elbow.

And, finally, she had spotted a bottle. It was small and amber-colored. Generic. But she knew well that it was meant to be a bottle of whiskey, the kind you pair with a can of Coke and drink behind the bleachers during a cold Autumn football game.

Lizzie could hear the water running in the bathroom and let herself in to find her friend. Ashley looked up at her from her spot at the sink. Mascara wove dark tracks down her face, which she was trying to clean with a scrap of wet paper towel.

"He sent you to babysit me?" Ashley groaned, still sniffling a bit.

"He sent me to help." Lizzie smiled and walked over to take the paper towel. "You might be making it worse with this thing. Do you keep any makeup in your bag?"

"I've got some powder?" She dug around in her bag and produced a small compact.

"That'll work." Lizzie gestured for Ashley to sit on the counter and set to work cleaning up the mess.

"Thank you," Ashley said. "I didn't mean to lose it like that. I think David is right. I'm just tired. I've been running myself ragged at work lately and then I come here and run myself ragged trying to sing and dance." She laughed, dry and unamused. "I'm an idiot."

"You're just doing your best." Lizzie dotted at her face with the pouf. "There. Much better."

Ashley slipped off the counter to look at her reflection. "You're a magician."

"It was an easy fix." Lizzie smiled at her.

"God," Ashley smacked a hand to her forehead. "I already blush every time I look David Flannery in the eye. Now it's going to be so much worse."

"Just imagine the kid in the *Godspell* t-shirt with the shag haircut," Lizzie laughed as she cleaned up the counter.

"How can I with that body?" Ashley moaned. "I can't believe you never jumped on that in high school. You two were inseparable. If anyone saw the potential, it had to be you."

"We were friends," she said, letting herself out of the bathroom as Ashley followed. "That was all. I mean, I guess there was once—"

"I *knew* it!" Ashley squealed and pulled her aside before the two could enter the stage door. "There's all this tension between the two of you. Freakin' Jim and Pam out there, even with Margo sitting right at the piano."

"There's no tension."

"What happened between the two of you?" Her eyes were big and round with curiosity.

Lizzie sighed. Ashley wasn't going to let this go. "I barely remember," she confessed. "He made a move, I rejected him, it's a story as old as time. I went to New York, and we never spoke again. If there's tension between the two of us it's because I left town pretty and popular and he was the charity case, but when I came back our roles were reversed." Lizzie crossed her arms. She could hear her voice cracking, betraying her true feelings.

"Graduation night?" Ashley asked.

"Lucky guess."

"I thought I remembered you two at Grace's party together. But weren't you with Ellis those days?"

Lizzie sighed and ran a hand through her hair to ease her mind. "It was a strange time."

"Well, you should move in on that," Ashley decided.

"I have a third date with Ellis this weekend, Ash." Lizzie laughed. "Besides, it seems like David has something going on with Margo, right? I'm happy for them. I really am. We don't have to be best friends for me to still support him."

Ashley put a dramatic hand to her breast in feigned emotion. "Ah, two gentlemen suitors to choose from. What a tough life Elizabeth Hancock leads!"

"I don't have two suitors," Lizzie laughed again as she

pushed the stage door open and "To Life" came blaring out at full volume. She lowered her voice to a whisper. "I'm not even positive that I have one. And David is still so angry with me for high school that he won't even look at me during rehearsal."

"Mhmm..." They slipped to the back of the group to join back into the number. "You're right. He's not looking at you. But it's taking every bit of focus he has." She grinned.

Lizzie rolled her eyes. "Just dance, Matchmaker."

Rehearsal finished up soon after. Clint and Grace joined the girls at the back of the stage, chugging from plastic water bottles and making plans to finally head over to Tequilas for once. They grabbed their bags from the stage wings and headed for the exit as Clint regaled the group with a story about how he'd mistakenly sung that their futures "be pheasant ones" instead of "pleasant ones."

From the corner of her eye, Lizzie saw David packing his own bag. He was talking with Margo, who had a hand on his elbow. Margo's long blonde hair shimmered under the hot stage lights as she leaned in to whisper something clever. David threw his head back in laughter and the happy sound carried over to where the group stood.

Lizzie felt a pang in her chest. She had to admit that she missed laughing with him that way. She hadn't thought about it in over a decade, but the memories of laughing and talking and drinking Jack and Coke behind the bleachers had all come flooding back in a quick thirty minutes.

And the memory of graduation night was there behind it all, too, pushing at the back of her brain, reminding her that it was a time that begged to be given attention once more.

"Looks like he's not the only one who is having trouble controlling his eyes," came Ashley's voice. She cackled.

CHAPTER 13

"This is kidnapping, Mr. Clarke."

"It's only kidnapping if I'm forcing you against your will."

Lizzie smiled as Ellis slipped his hand into hers over the car console. "You told Poppy you were giving me a lift to rehearsal. I definitely don't have rehearsal."

Ellis shrugged, cool and confident. "Doesn't mean that you aren't still going to be practicing something while you're away." He winked at her and she smacked his arm in faux horror.

"You left a feeble old man to watch a bunch of children. Lest you forget, that's literally my *job*."

"Small price to pay." He swung the Lexus into a parking lot and stopped the car under the shade of a massive oak tree. He'd taken her to his house.

When Lizzie and her father weren't living in a trailer or crashing on a relative's couch, they were staying in Shady Lane apartments. The drab olive and gray buildings had been put up in the seventies, and looked like they might fall over if the right hurricane came along. Lizzie distinctly remembered a leak in the ceiling that management had "temporarily" fixed by placing a trash can under the drip. Shady Lane was, however, the standard of Warner Robins apartment living. While the Haves of the city lived in neighborhoods like Nora's, the Have-Nots lived like Lizzie and her father, making do with the old, the tired, and the forgotten places like Shady Lane.

Ellis Clarke's apartment complex was decidedly *not* Shady Lane.

Here, on the outskirts of Macon, was what must be the only new complex Lizzie had ever heard of being built in Warner Robins. The buildings looked almost shiny with their cream paint and pristine windows. Lizzie saw puppies and their posh owners walking clean, white sidewalks instead of latchkey children playing in the dirt. She wondered if any of the tenants here had ever heard a dish being thrown against their neighbor's wall. Maybe just if the neighbor was frustrated that the plate didn't match their newly redecorated kitchen ...

"I'm on the third floor," Ellis said as he let himself out of the car. He pulled open her door to let her out.

"I need the exercise. Stairs will be good for me."

Ellis laughed. "We'll just take the elevator." *Yeesh.* "It opens up right to each private apartment, so easy." *Double yeesh.*

They walked up to the building where Ellis keyed in a code to let them in. The doors swung open to reveal the elevator. "Jeez, this thing is really private?" Lizzie asked with wide eyes. "How much does this place cost?! Maybe I should have gone to law school—"

But she never finished the thought. Before the doors had even shut, Ellis had pushed her up against the elevator wall. His mouth, warm and pressing, was urgent on her neck.

Lizzie felt the heat rush up to her cheeks as his hands found their way into her back pockets.

"El ..." She wanted to sound authoritative. She knew she sounded conquered. "I really can't leave Poppy alone for long..."

As the elevator doors swung open to his foyer, Ellis whisked her out and pressed her up against a new wall. With a hand at the back of her head, he pulled her close. Despite the signs that it was coming, the kiss still took Lizzie off guard. His lips pressed against hers and for a wanton, animal moment she was totally swept away by desire.

He pressed his forehead to hers, breathing deeply. She could see that his eyes were still closed. "I've been wanting to do that since the moment I first saw you at that coffee shop."

She had forgotten how good it could be with Ellis. In high school, everything seems good. It's a time full of firsts and experimentation. Every first date is a dream. Every first kiss a fantasy. Lizzie had been with other men in New Jersey. And they'd been good, too. They had treated her well. She had even worked up the guts to introduce one to her kids. Somewhere along the line she had blurred Ellis in with the others, assuming that time had exaggerated how good things were with him. Just as the memories of their breakup had been warped and faded, so had the memory of his charm and allure.

Now, though ... they fit together like she had never left at all. There was a connection there, something physical and carnal that went beyond the simple joys of high school first crushes. And for the millionth time, she questioned why they had ever broken up in the first place. His need for her was imperative. It was demanding. And as a grown woman, she found that perhaps she liked it.

Something sparked in the back of her mind. A moment, frozen in place, near-perfectly preserved. Ellis' hands on her neck the same way they were in his foyer. Pressing deep into her skin. Maybe too deep. Ellis Clarke had always taken what he'd wanted. She had spent so much time after that night thinking that maybe he had been possessive. Thinking she had missed the signs of an underlying darkness. A violence.

But she had changed in ten years, and as she felt his fingertips at her throat now, urging her closer, she felt a shift in her perspective. What was once possession she now saw as a dominance that perhaps she could desire. What was once brutality she now saw as his vulnerable, powerful need for her, splayed out before her as his strongest craving.

Perhaps this was the distorted memories finally coming back into focus. She had dreaded returning home for so long, but maybe doing so had helped her to see things as they really were. She could stop questioning the meaning of that night that happened so long ago. She could stop feeling guilty for it and move on.

Yes, Ellis Clarke had always taken what he'd wanted. She pocketed the thought, pleased with herself for growing and changing as he had. He could have her if he wanted. Hell, he could have all of her. She determined that she wasn't the kind of girl who would run away this time.

He started for the buttons on her shirt and she giggled, nerves finally getting the best of her. "El, really. Poppy is—"

"Poppy will figure it out," he murmured in her ear, throwing her down on his couch.

Lizzie felt her phone go off in her pocket. She pulled it out and pressed it up to his chest, half-smiling at him in victory. "I told you I'm needed. Buttons back on, sir. Besides, it's only our third time out. Don't you want a little mystery?"

Ellis took the phone from her, grinning with flashing white teeth as he slipped it into his back pocket. "Forget mystery. I waited ten years to find you, I can't wait any longer."

He stopped short, groaning, to retrieve the phone from his pocket. It was buzzing again. The screen lit up. POPPY. He tossed it, and the phone skidded across his carpet to rest by the coffee table. Ellis returned to his task, busying himself with little kisses on Lizzie's neck that sent goose-bumps up her skin.

Buzz. Buzz. The phone went off again, rattling loud against the foot of the coffee table.

"Son of a—" Ellis sat up in a huff, running an impatient hand through his hair. He motioned with a flipped hand for Lizzie to answer.

"I'm so sorry," she placated, picking up the phone. Her fingers were trembling as she started in on her buttons. "Poppy?"

"Elizabeth, praise the Lord." Poppy's voice was breathy and frantic. Lizzie's stomach soured. "You have to come home. There's been an accident. Nora. It's Nora. She was hit by a car down near the high school."

"Hit by a car?" The words sounded strange and unreal being said aloud. "What was she even doing by the high school? Her office is clear across town—"

"There's no time to explain," Poppy answered. "The kids are waiting here for you. I have to go now."

"Ok, ok." Lizzie stood up, quickly finishing up buttoning her blouse and gathering her things where they were scattered across the floor. She mouthed an apology to Ellis, who nodded and grabbed his car keys once more.

Traffic was light, and the car ride was fast. "You're sure

you don't need me to come in with you?" Ellis asked her as she let herself out of the Lexus.

"I don't want to have to explain this to my kids yet," she answered, her face screwed up in apology. She leaned in to give him a quick kiss on the cheek. "Try again later?"

"Try again later," he agreed.

She ran inside, letting herself in through the back deck. "Fullmer? Hazel?" The kitchen was empty, but she heard noises coming from the den down the hall. "Caroline? I hope you haven't been here by yourselves for too long—"

She stopped short in the doorway. Fullmer ran up to her, his face glowing with excitement. "He fixed it, Mom! Listen, the Coltrane is playing right again!"

Lizzie's stomach dropped as she saw David Flannery push himself up off the den floor. He bent down to retrieve his sweater from Hazel, but Lizzie could see that his face was just as flushed as hers must be.

"What are you doing here?" She asked.

"Poppy called me," he explained. "Bill couldn't get through Macon traffic fast enough, and Poppy thought you were at rehearsal. I offered to help out until you could get here."

"Mom, you have to listen to the Village Vanguard stuff!" Fullmer was practically hopping as he fiddled with his old record player. Music rushed up at the group in a garbled mess that Lizzie still couldn't comprehend.

"David has been telling us high school stories about you." Hazel's eyes were lit up with her own excitement.

"Too many, I'm sure." She offered up a sympathetic smile to David, but he didn't take the olive branch. Instead, he pulled on his wool cardigan and started toward the door.

"I've gotta get going, guys," he said. He stopped to

whisper in her ear. "I'd appreciate it if you didn't use me as your excuse again."

"David, no!" Caroline grabbed his leg, clinging to the black jeans.

"It's bedtime, baby girl," Lizzie said, scooping a yawning Caroline up into her arms. "You've been up late enough as it is."

"Tell me a bedtime story, David!" she whined.

"Jeez, you've really done a number on them."

"I've really got to get going..."

Fullmer, Hazel, and Mary-Kate joined in Caroline's chorus, tugging at his sleeves. "David, c'mon! We want to hear more stories about you and Mom!"

David looked at Lizzie, searching for an out. If he wasn't going to take her first olive branch, she wasn't going to give him another. "C'mon, David," she said. "The kids just want to hear a few more stories."

CHAPTER 14

The whole house was dark by the time David and Lizzie had finished getting all the kids in bed. The Hancock and Grant-Thornton kids had fought until the end, asking for "Just one more story, *please!*" over and over until one of the adults would relent at last. Sleep had overtaken Fullmer last of all and he had closed his eyes snuggled into the crook of David's arm, a smile still on his lips from listening to the last tale from high school.

"They're still not back." Lizzie glanced out the front window as they arrived back downstairs. She saw no headlights indicating a return home from the hospital. "I hope Nora's okay. I hate not being there with her. Did Poppy tell you anything?"

"Just that she looked like she had a broken or sprained arm, but that it wasn't anything that would kill her."

"Thank God," Lizzie sighed with a hand to her heart. "That's more detail than I got."

"He was really freaking out when he called the Baron," David said.

Lizzie was grateful for the darkness as she felt the blush

creep back onto her face. "David, I'm so sorry about that. I was—"

"You don't have to explain where you were." His voice was curt again, the same professional tones he used in the theater. He draped his cardigan over one arm and started for the front door. "I'll see you at rehearsal tomorrow. *Real* rehearsal." He opened the door.

"Don't go." She stopped him with a hand on his forearm. The gesture surprised both of them. In the moon's pale, milky light streaking through the doorway, she could just see that her fingertips brushed the amber bottle of whiskey inked on his skin. "Let me make you a drink. It's the least I can do."

His eyes searched hers as he thought for a second. "...Okay," he said, shutting the door. His answer surprised her as much as her original offer had.

Lizzie flipped on a lamp to light their way to the kitchen. "Thanks for fixing Fullmer's record player. He's been complaining about it running backwards for a while now."

"I don't know what I did, but it's working now." David shrugged. "You really can't tell if it's running forwards or backwards?"

"Ugh, it all sounds like gibberish notes to me."

A small smile cracked David's tough facade. "God, Lizzie, how were we ever friends? All I ever played in my car back in high school was Davis, Ellington, or Coltrane."

"I can't believe I forgot about that." She shook her head in disbelief. They had made it to the kitchen. She flipped on the overhead light, enjoying the warm, comforting glow reflecting off the black granite countertops. "I'm glad you were here tonight. Thank you." She gestured to a stool for David as she let herself in to the liquor cabinet. "There's one thing I didn't forget about: Jack and Coke, coming right up."

"Man, I haven't had one of those in forever. I don't drink too much anymore. No time, what with running the theater."

"Really?" Lizzie asked as she opened up the fridge to grab a can of soda. "I thought with your tattoo—"

A pale blush made its way up from under David's beard, leaving his cheeks a rosy red as he averted his eyes. "Ah, you saw that one."

"It's kind of a—" Lizzie gestured wildly with her arms, indicating the far-reaching extent of his sleeve tattoos "—big change since high school. Who could miss it?"

"I think most people just get lost in the ink," he shrugged. "Not too many people catch the individual stuff."

She poured him a glass and slid it across the counter, then poured her own. They paused the conversation, both taking deep drinks from their cups.

"What's it for?" She asked. "I mean, why the sleeves?"

"They are ... reminders." David's eyes were lost in his drink. He took another swig, long and deep. Despite his casual tone, his face was giving him away: he looked like he'd rather be anywhere else but alone, talking to Lizzie.

"Reminders?"

"I get one for each thing I wish I could go back and change. I don't really want to redo time. I think it's silly to live in the past. This way, I feel a sense of loss or regret and I get a tattoo. Let the ink be a reminder to change in the future. To fix things for myself."

"And the bottle of Jack Daniels—"

"Is exactly what you think it is." David looked her in the eye now. "It was the first one I got. It was the first reminder to never make the same mistake again."

Lizzie's breath caught in her throat. "I was a mistake?"

Silence hung heavy in the air between them. David's

eyes turned stony and unwavering. "You were my best friend, Lizzie." He cleared his throat. His face contorted with a pain she felt she could now understand. "But I didn't want that. I never wanted that. I thought you knew ... well, even if you didn't know before, it had to be clear after graduation night."

The words weren't coming easy to Lizzie. She had bottled away this conversation a million times over the years, placed it on the shelf for a later time. Now, the right thing to say was eluding her. She didn't know what to add, so she stuck to the facts. "That night was your first time ..." She started slow, cautious. He nodded, taking another long swig of his drink. "I was your first, then I disappeared, and you never heard from me again. You're probably right to call it a mistake, but it wasn't yours. It was mine. After prom when Ellis and I... well, after we..."

The words still weren't coming out the way that she wanted them to, but she pressed on, trying to find her own answers as she finally gave voice to what had happened between them. "You and I just got so close those few weeks after prom. Looking back, hooking up on graduation night seems kind of inevitable, but I certainly shouldn't have..."

This time when the words wouldn't come, she let the sentence fade off into the ether. There was too much to be said between them. The air hung heavy with unspoken words. Finally, David broke the silence.

"I couldn't believe it was you when you showed up at the Baron for auditions. Somehow you got prettier since high school. I didn't even want to look at you."

"Are you kidding?" Lizzie said in disbelief. "So says the man who looks like he took up weight-lifting with Wolverine while I was gone?"

David smiled, sheepish. "I spent a lot of time trying to

get better from my mistake. You can thank my reminder ink for any weight loss, business ownership, or other personal successes. I'm thinking of patenting my system."

"You're a catch, David Flannery. Every girl at your theater thinks so. Margo is lucky to have you."

David laughed. "Margo?" he asked, incredulous. He chuckled again and threw back another swallow of whiskey. "Margo and I are just friends. We were, um, maybe friends with a few more benefits at one point, but we aren't together now."

Lizzie raised her eyebrows and crossed her arms. David threw up his arms in faux exasperation. "I met her in musical theater back in college. We could relate. I had just lost my best friend, and she had lost her fiancé. It was a car accident."

Lizzie's hand went to her heart. "That's awful."

"She had a string of bad boyfriends after. Really bad. And one of them... well, I'm sure you could relate to her, too. We were there for each other through some hard times. But Margo is just a friend."

Lizzie cleared her throat and shifted her weight from one foot to the other.

"I'm sorry." David's apology hung in the air between them. "I haven't been kind to you. Margo has reminded me of that at every rehearsal."

Lizzie laughed, the sound hollow and empty. "I'm not sure I deserve your kindness, anyway."

"I could hardly look at you in rehearsal. I had built you up in my mind to be someone calloused or awful or even ugly. But you weren't. You definitely weren't." David crossed his arms, his eyes on the ground once more.

"I figured you hated me." She swallowed, a hard lump forming in her throat.

"No," he admitted. "I couldn't hate you. But I also couldn't let myself get wrapped up in you again. I agreed to let you in the show because I couldn't stand to just let you disappear from my life altogether again, but then I couldn't string together a single sentence around you because I couldn't stand to let you back into my heart either. Kind of messed up and complicated, huh?"

Lizzie could feel herself blushing again. She cleared her throat and turned to pour more Coke, hoping that he wouldn't look her in the face. "I'm familiar with complicated."

"I don't make the same mistakes twice," he continued quietly. "The tattoos remind me of that. But one of those mistakes I shouldn't make again is letting you walk away. What happened between us is in the past. I think I want to move on."

She looked at him, more than a little taken off guard. "I'd like that very much."

"I don't do grumpy and distant very well," David said with a small smile. "I think I'm going to give myself an aneurism if I keep straining to ignore all the things I used to like about you."

He extended his hand. The gesture took Lizzie by surprise. She reached out and grabbed his hand to shake it. "Friends?" she asked.

He nodded, smiling.

"It seems we sort of have to be friends now anyway," he said, passing his empty glass back to her. "I think your kids might like me better than you." He threw up his hands, feigning arrogance.

"Oh, please." Lizzie rolled her eyes, smiling back at him. "They like anyone who will rat out their mom's high school secrets."

"Fullmer and I may have discussed the incident when your braces got stuck in the back of Emily Amherst's hair..."

"Come on!" She laughed. It felt good.

"He's a great kid." David smiled and picked up the whiskey to pour himself another glass. Lizzie felt a warmth spread from her chest. He was going to stay a while longer. "Hazel is, too. She's a firecracker, that kid. Must get it from her mama."

"Spitting image," Lizzie said. "It's hard on Fullmer. He feels left out of the party. He's always been a little—"

"Rad? I've never met a kid that likes jazz. I mean I *did*, but that's technically only because I was always hanging out with you and Nora, and Poppy only ever played the good stuff at his house. I was kind of indoctrinated. But Fullmer! Man. You raised that kid right, Hancock. Don't know how since he decidedly did *not* get his taste in music from you. Thank God he isn't obsessed with The Cranberries."

He stuck out his tongue in distaste, and Lizzie laughed. "Come on! They're a highly respected musical group."

"Please." David grinned. "Ya know, I've got a friend that plays jazz who will be in the city this weekend. He's playing at The Red Dirt. I know it's a bar, but I'm friends with the owner and I'm sure we could sneak the kids in for a bit if they wanted to maybe listen and—"

"Fullmer would love that. I mean, *love* that." Lizzie agreed. "Count us in. And Poppy, too. You know he'll invite himself, anyway."

"I wouldn't have it any other way," David said. He placed his glass in the sink and picked up his sweater to head out. "I can pick you all up after the kids get out of school this Friday? We could caravan over?"

"That sounds wonderful."

"Okay, good then. I'll let myself out. Thanks again for the

drink." David waved and headed out of the kitchen to the front door.

Lizzie leaned back against the countertop, her mind far away from the little kitchen. Without her having even noticed it, her tiny security bubble she'd built up around her children had begun to dissolve away. She hadn't seen David Flannery in years before *Fiddler*, and yet they'd somehow made plans to go out with her kids over the course of one honest conversation. It was a big deal!

She rarely worried about Hazel. Boy craze aside, the kid knew how to be social and take care of herself. But when it came to Fullmer, Lizzie usually had a few lines of explanation ready for friends and strangers who asked too many questions. She was so used to rushing to his defense, to rationalizing his various ticks and mannerisms.

But there'd been no need for that with David. He hadn't put Lizzie on the defense. He hadn't even asked the usual questions. He'd liked her son, accepted him fully, and wanted to include him in something fun and... *ordinary*. Lizzie was so taken aback by the invitation to The Red Dirt that she hardly knew how to feel. Her skin was buzzing. Her eyes were unsure where to focus. And she smiled—big and broad and surprisingly relaxed.

Lizzie hopped up on the counter and poured herself a glass of whiskey, no Coke. She took it in both hands, throwing her head back to chug it. She relished the burning feeling in her throat as the drink made its way down.

CHAPTER 15

"Go ahead, pinch me." Nora grinned at Margo, who shook her head in absolution.

"No freakin' way. Do I look a sadist? Do I have horns at the back of my head that no one ever told me about, David?"

"No horns," David smiled as he brought over drinks for the group. "But you probably ought to do something about that spiked tail."

"C'mon," Nora whined. "Pinch me. I'm totally tough. It was barely a sprain at all."

"You're wearing a sling," Lizzie noted.

"As your doctor and your father, I'm exercising my authority now to tell you not to be stupid." Poppy chimed in, grabbing his drink. "I like to tell myself that I raised you better."

"Can it, retiree. I'm proving my strength! Pinch me, woman!"

Margo giggled, hesitant. Finally, she gave in and pinched Nora's forearm.

"God, *why*?" Nora squealed, babying her sprained arm.

But the charade didn't last long before she broke, her own laughter giving her away. "See? Totally fine. It was no big deal. I'm basically a badass."

"Auntie Nora, language!"

"Thank you, Hazel." Lizzie smiled and elbowed Nora. "I still don't understand what you were doing by the high school."

"Errands," Nora shrugged, taking her drink from David.

"I thought Lizzie was your errand girl," he said, passing around the rest of the order.

"I am," Lizzie noted, her voice cross.

"Mom, Mom, Mom! It's starting!" Fullmer tugged on her sleeve. His eyes were all wonder and awe, lit up sparkling blue by the sweeping stage lights. "I can't see..."

"No prob, Bob." David passed Margo his drink and scooped up Fullmer to sit on his shoulders. Lizzie couldn't help but smile as she watched her son counting the number of musicians in the band under his breath.

She felt a hand at her waist and looked down to see Hazel also in wonder. Her blue eyes lit up as she stared, transfixed, at the stage. Lizzie scooped her up and put her daughter on her own shoulders, so both children could watch the show. They'd always had to take turns before, with Lizzie divvying up her attention from the first days they came home, tiny and pink, from the hospital. It felt good to see them both getting a moment to themselves. She squeezed Hazel's small fingertips as her daughter absent-mindedly played with the back of her hair.

All at once, the music started in loud and brassy. The horns came in, fast and aggressive, followed by drums that beat a pulse through the floorboards. It was big band music at its absolute finest, whipping the room up into a frenzy of excitement. A girlish giggle escaped Lizzie's lips when she saw Poppy shuffling to the beat. His mouth split wide into a ridiculous grin. He put a hand to his daughter's back and scooped her close to his body, holding her to his chest as he swirled around to the music.

Fullmer was lost in the magic. His eyes were transfixed on the stage and his small hands gripped David's shoulders with white knuckles. His mouth hung up in a quirky half-smile, his face frozen that way as he watched the musicians at work. Suddenly he looked down at Lizzie, his spellbound expression cracking into a grin of wild excitement.

"Mom! This is so great!"

Lizzie reached over and squeezed his knee. She could feel a strong beat in her fingers and toes and she knew that it was from her own heart rather than the amped up jazz. For the first time in her life, the music was starting to make sense. She felt it resonate inside her, filling her up and bubbling out in a laugh she could not contain. Maybe she still wasn't her son's Coltrane expert. But she could enjoy the here and now. She liked it.

The concert was over far too soon. The sax player, sweat pouring out from under his cocked newsboy cap, waved an exhausted goodbye to the crowd as he led the band in a final, quieter number to play out the audience. David let Fullmer down from his shoulders. The boy rushed over to Lizzie as she let Hazel down. He hugged her knees at full strength in his enthusiasm.

"That was *amazing!*" he cried.

"Yeah, it was totally cool." Hazel agreed. Her little cheeks were flushed bright pink with excitement.

"Wanna go meet the musicians?" David asked him.

Fullmer's eyes somehow grew even bigger. "Mom, can I?"

"Did you think I'd say no?" Lizzie laughed. "Take me with you!"

Poppy shuffled forward to grab David's arm. "If you leave an old man behind, I will write you all out of my will!"

"Come on," David said, laughing. He led the group through the crowd, dodging waitresses and drunken patrons to head around to the side of the stage. He waved his arms up at the sax player. "Oy! Sanders!"

The musician turned around to see the group waiting there. His face broke into a smile as he pulled off his instrument and removed his hat, revealing a thick head of dripping wet red hair. "Flannery! So glad you could make it, man!"

"I've got some folks I want you to meet," David said, pushing Fullmer forward. "Sanders, meet Hazel and Lizzie Hancock and Anton and Nora Grant. And can't forget Fullmer here. Kid is going to put you out of work in a few years."

"You're a sax player?" Sanders knelt down to sit on the edge of the stage.

Fullmer nodded, speech escaping him for a few seconds. "I only know a little."

"Kid's a prodigy," Poppy interjected, winking and squeezing Fullmer's shoulders. The boy's face turned bright red as a smile overtook his face. "He just started playing, but he was already featured in his school's musical."

"Nice," Sanders said, nodding with enthusiasm. "That's where I started. Gotta sweat it out in the pit before you can be the star of the show." His gaze fell on Lizzie and his face lit up. He ran a hand through his sweaty hair and stuck it out for her to shake. "And who is this enchanting creature, David?"

"That's just my mom," Fullmer said, waving off the question. "Can I look at your sax?"

"Lizzie Hancock," she answered, shaking his hand.

"Sure, you can look at my sax, little buddy." Sanders swung his heavy instrument around. "You wanna take a look, too, doll?"

David pushed between them. "Hey, did I introduce you to my friend Margo at any of your shows before?"

David pulled her up. Margo tripped as she stepped toward Sanders, landing with both hands square on his chest.

"I'm so sorry," she apologized, her blonde hair sweeping forward as she covered her face in embarrassment.

"No worries at all." Sanders was starry-eyed, his attentions for Lizzie all but forgotten. "Say, sweetheart, have you ever seen a green room before?"

"And that's our cue to bail," David whispered in Lizzie's ear. "Best not get in the way of Sanders on the warpath. Fullmer, Hazel, do you think you can stay up just a little bit more past your bedtime for karaoke?"

Both kids' eyes were dinner plates. "*Mom*?"

Lizzie shrugged. "I'm already the bad parent who brought my kids into a bar. What's an hour or two of staying up past bedtime?"

The group made their way back into the bar and found seats around a small square table. "I'll grab some waters!" Nora volunteered, pulling out a chair for Poppy before she made her way back to the bartender.

"So, what did you think?" David asked Fullmer.

"AWESOME!" The kid exploded with excitement. "He was so fast! And did you hear that improv? The other guys couldn't even keep up! I've got to start practicing more, Mom. Do you think I can take lessons?"

Lizzie laughed. "Let's just focus on breathing for now."

"And you, Hazel? What did you like?" David asked.

"Did you see the boy who brought them their drinks after?" Hazel had gone starry-eyed as she tracked a young waiter walking the perimeter of the bar. "He's so cu-ute!"

Lizzie felt the gut instinct to chime in and remind her daughter of the waiter's age, but was surprised when David jumped in instead. "Whoa, Hazel, talk about being into older men!" His face had grown beet red. Was he embarrassed? Lizzie chuckled. "I can't let you turn into a sugar baby or your mom will never let me see you again. Back away from the waiter."

Hazel giggled into her hands and pushed David playfully on the arm.

"Fullmer, I was thinking. I can teach you some more of the basics." Poppy offered. He sat back in his chair, eyes half closed, fully relaxed. It was the most at peace that Lizzie had ever seen him. "I think I've even still got some old sheet music sitting around."

"That would be so cool! Do you have any Coltrane?" Fullmer was tapping Poppy's arm, but the old man didn't seem to notice. He had sat back up, his eyes scanning the wall of the bar.

Lizzie turned to see what he was looking at. Nora was standing in the crowd, her arms laden heavy with cups of water. She had a confused look on her face and she looked at the waters as though she had never meant to pick them up. Poppy got up, his movements suddenly swift and purposeful. "Be right back," he muttered. Lizzie watched as he made his way over to Nora, putting a hand on the small of her back and leaning down to whisper in her ear. She still looked puzzled and Lizzie watched as she reached out her long, thin fingers to brush the gray whiskers on Poppy's chin.

"Hey, they just put out the karaoke sign-up sheet!" David's voice broke Lizzie's concentration. She turned back to the table where David was elbowing her son. "Gonna sing something for us, musical prodigy?"

Fullmer's ears turned bright red. "Do I have to?"

"Oh, no!" David covered. He waved over the waiter who had the sheet just as Poppy returned with Nora to distribute glasses of water around the table. "I'm sure your mom has been dying to go first, anyway."

Fullmer's embarrassment turned quickly to enthusiasm. "Yeah, Mom! Sing for us!"

"I would need about two more drinks for that," she laughed.

"Excuses, excuses," David said. "You sing all the time in rehearsal. Come on, you're great!"

He reached out and squeezed her hand. It was a small gesture. She was sure he didn't mean it as anything much. Still, Lizzie felt a little flip in her stomach. Somehow she had bridged the gap between them. Somehow they had made up for the lost time. She felt something stir within her, something that had lain dormant for so long. She wanted to reach out and touch his face. Feel the thick of his hair. The delicate silk of his skin.

As before with Ellis, a moment near-perfectly preserved buoyed up in her mind's eye. A young David, unsure but eager, holding her close. Asking if it was okay to touch her. Asking if it was okay if she touched him. He had smelled like the Baron did now, like ancient pine and earthy cotton. She had relished in its safety and security as he unzipped her graduation dress. As he had kissed her neck, slow and yearning.

"I'll go first then," David shrugged, breaking her concentration once more.

"Go first?" Nora looked confused.

"Karaoke, sugar." Poppy put an arm around her shoulders.

"No one else has signed up yet," the waiter explained. "Mic's all yours."

David set himself steady and took a gulp from his water cup. "That would be so much better if it was whiskey," he murmured to Lizzie.

He stood up, and the table cheered. Fullmer yelled the loudest. David made his way up to the mic, which he covered to say something quietly to the karaoke machine operator. "Alright, Fullmer," he said as the music cued up. "If I can embarrass myself like this then you can, too."

An eighties synth beat blasted through the speakers, taking everyone in the room by surprise. A few nervous giggles could be heard as drunken patrons started to bop their heads.

"*We're talking away. I don't know what I'm to say.*" David's voice, broken and off-rhythm, blasted through the room. "*I'll say it, anyway. Today's another day to find you.*"

Fullmer put both of his hands over his ears, his face sour. "Is something wrong?" He yelled over the music.

Lizzie laughed and laughed, her belly rocking. "He's tone-deaf! I completely forgot."

David was as committed as ever, blasting his way through to the challenging chorus of a-ha's iconic "Take on Me." When the highest note came, he stood on his toes, his face screwed up as he belted.

"*In a day or twooooo!*"

The whole table was roaring with laughter as Margo and Sanders the sax player came over to join them. Sanders took a swig of the drink in his hand. "This is always the risk you run when you invite David Flannery for a night out."

Margo crossed her arms, smiling. "Hey, I won't complain. It's why he hired a full-time music director for his theater."

Sanders put an arm around her shoulders, pulling her lean body close to his. Lizzie smiled and breathed a sigh of relief that she hadn't realized she'd been holding.

$\sim$

*E*arly on a Saturday morning, the state of the world outside made Lizzie question whether she had overstayed her welcome in Warner Robins.

The sky was gray and weepy. Clouds hung low and fogged to expose unwashed windows. The trees on the Grant-Thornton property hung heavy with tiny, spiked icicles that threatened to fall and stab anyone who dared walk on the frosted grass. The unforgiving nature dared to follow guests inside with tracks of slushy brown mud that flicked off of rain boots and clung onto furniture and walls.

The air in the house was pressing and stuffy. Bill had fiddled with the thermostat all morning, debating between keeping it off and running the heat. Whichever he chose turned out to be wrong: the house stayed at a near-constant stifle, made worse by the sweaty bodies of cooped-up children running through the halls.

Lizzie packed up for her last dress rehearsal before *Fiddler* opened. As she headed into the kitchen to grab a last-minute snack, she spied Bill and Poppy reading newspapers at the table, looking utterly miserable as the sounds of a raucous game of freeze tag echoed into the room. She waved a sheepish goodbye, feeling both sorry for them and glad for her own escape.

"Pity us," Bill groaned, not bothering to even lower his paper.

"Looove you!" Lizzie darted out the back door. The chill of the air took her aback. The cold bit through her sweatshirt, sending a shiver down her spine. She slogged through the thick, muddy clay to the driveway, feeling beyond grateful for the safety of the borrowed Camry.

At rehearsal, the rest of the cast echoed Lizzie's sentiments. The dressing room was near silent, save for the sounds of sniffles and muffled coughs as a reminder of the treachery outside. Lizzie found her spot in front of the mirror and plopped her bag on the counter. Foundation and lipstick rolled out, clanging across the linoleum. The other girls jumped.

"Sorry!" Lizzie winced.

"Don't apologize," Grace waved her off from the other end of the mirror. "We all need to perk up, anyway. Right, ladies?" A few moans came in response.

A knock sounded at the door. "Come in!" Grace called.

Margo's blonde head peeked through the crack. "Everybody dressed?" She let herself in, shutting the door quietly behind her. She settled into a chair next to Lizzie, brandishing some sheet music. "Keep getting ready; don't mind me. I just came to talk about the changes David wants at the end of 'Do You Love Me.'"

"I know," Lizzie said, beginning to apply her makeup. "Back off a little on the last note. Hold it for a beat longer."

"You're the best," Margo smiled. "Can I help you with anything else? I've got all this time to kill while everyone gets ready."

"Hang out with us," Lizzie volunteered. "I think we could all use the company."

"Ugh, I have no energy," Grace bemoaned. Her mouth

was open in a perfect O as she applied her lipstick, but she kept trying to talk despite it. "This weather is killin' me. I need some wakin' up!"

The young girl sitting next to Lizzie perked up. "Do you think Mr. Flannery would let us drink some coffee?"

"In these handmade costumes? Dream on." Lizzie snorted.

"I can go talk to him," Margo offered. "I know he gets grumpy around showtime, but he usually listens to reason when caffeine is at stake."

"You two are so close. How did you meet again?" Lizzie already knew the answer. So why was she bothering to ask the question? She watched from the corner of her eye as the tall blonde shifted in her seat.

"We both went to Macon State. We were in the Musical Theater program."

"David Flannery used to sing?" Grace interjected, her eyebrows raised with disbelief as she applied some blush.

"Ha! Definitely not." Margo chuckled. "Back then he thought he was going to do the tech track. I talked him into directing later down the road."

"And you guys used to date, right?" The question was coming out of Lizzie's mouth before she could stop herself. She felt a natural blush blooming on her cheeks before she ever bothered applying any. She shouldn't feel so curious. Ellis flashed into her mind, tall, dashing, charming as ever. Plainly wanting her. Lizzie stiffened her back and her resolve.

"No," Margo answered. "Not really. We were just kind of there at the right time, in the right place for each other. I had a fiancé who died in a car accident. And he was ... going through his own stuff."

Lizzie could feel Margo's eyes on the back of her head as

she continued applying her makeup, and she determined not to turn back and look.

"Anyway, we were there for each other when we both needed a friend. I started dating some guys. None of them any good." Margo's voice broke. Lizzie couldn't help herself; she turned around to see Margo's face. Her brown eyes had hardened, transfixed on her hands clasped in her lap. Her mouth turned down at the corners, threatening to break at any moment. "There was one guy ... he was really bad."

The room grew quiet. Grace walked across the room to put a hand on Margo's shoulder. "You don't have to talk about it, hon."

Margo shook her off. Her face hardened into a look of resolution. "No, it's okay. I spent a lot of time feeling like what happened between us was my fault. Like I had done something to deserve the way that he treated me." She laughed, the sound bitter and hollow. "Hell, at the time I didn't even report him for what happened between us. I could have ruined his life. So much would be different now..." Margo's voice drifted off, and she looked very far away. Finally, the resolution hardened in her eyes, and she cleared her throat. "But I'm not staying silent anymore. If I don't acknowledge what he did, it's like I'm giving him back some of that power over me that he wanted. I'm letting him win."

The room was silent. Lizzie knew better than to speak. Her curiosity was bordering on morbid. It didn't matter if David Flannery was friends with Margo or more than friends or if he had even used her as a replacement for a month back in college after Lizzie had bailed. Margo's story wasn't anything to her. She had Ellis now, and he wanted her, *really* wanted her, and—

"What did that guy do to you?" Well, she couldn't take the words back now.

The lights in the room flashed. The overhead speakers crackled as David's voice came over the intercom. "Places, everybody. We run in five."

"Well," Grace swooped over to the door, brushing breezily past Lizzie's awkward question that still hung in the air. "Anyone wanna come do some vocal warmups in the east wing?"

The group of girls stood and started to shuffle out, many still groaning about their lack of energy. Lizzie stood, too, grabbing her costume from the rack and pulling it over her head. When she turned to go, she was surprised to see Margo standing by the door.

The girl folded her arms. Her eyes were fixed on a spot on the floor. "I told him no. All night I told him that I was inexperienced, that I wanted to wait before I was with a man again. But he said he got what he wanted. Kept acting like I was going to like being with him. He raped me on a Tuesday night. He raped me on a Tuesday, and only David was there to help me pick up the pieces."

She reached out and gripped Lizzie's arm. Her long, slender fingers pressed into her skin, urgent and needing.

"I'm so sorry, Margo. I shouldn't have asked you something so personal." Lizzie's voice was quiet.

Margo looked up at her then, her eyes wet. Her full pink lips softened into a bare smile. "If I stay silent, it's like I never get to say how wrong he was." She squeezed Lizzie's arm again. She paused, choosing her next words with plain care. "David missed you, Lizzie. I was a fix for a while. Something we both needed in the moment. He was there for me in every way he could be... but he never once forgot about you."

Lizzie was hyperaware of the stifling heat in the dressing room. The yellow lights reflected off the mirrors, burning into her arms. She fanned herself, feeling grateful that the gesture might shield her face just a little bit. "I think I need to step outside for a bit before the show starts," she said. "Get some of that cold air."

CHAPTER 16

"*I* can't believe you never had filet mignon before." Ellis was grinning at Lizzie, arms crossed as he leaned back in his chair.

"What can I say? I hear they don't cook well on the tiny trailer park stovetops." She smiled back.

It was their latest date out, the last they could squeeze in before Lizzie's chaotic tech week rehearsals and the first round of shows. Ellis had picked her up at Nora's home dressed in a blue sharkskin suit. The top two buttons of his grey shirt were undone, revealing a bare hint of tanned collarbone that had sent Lizzie's stomach into tumbles. She'd chosen her own outfit carefully, going with a short, sleek black dress. It was the only thing that had felt remotely nice enough to wear to Valentino's, the Italian restaurant that was their destination for the evening. She had stressed about the pick all day, regretting with intensity the lack of time she spent on exercise as well as her skin's predisposition for extreme paleness.

Ellis had presented her with a single red rose, which Nora had gushed over even more than Lizzie had. It had been placed with care in a glass vase on the kitchen table before Ellis swooped his date out the door and down the driveway to his car. Lizzie was floating in her own fantasy world the whole drive over to Valentino's.

In the restaurant, Ellis' preparation had shown through once more. They had a small table tucked away in a private corner, a fact which Lizzie had noted with relief as she remembered the flirting waitress from Cubano's. He'd pulled out the chair for her before she sat down, and she got a high off the woody, opulent scent of his cologne. His order was generous, including not just the filet mignon but also a full bottle of expensive red wine and a delicate chocolate dessert that took an hour ahead of eating to prepare.

Lizzie sat back in her chair, hands on her belly. "If you keep stuffing me like this, you'll get to see what I looked like when I was pregnant with the twins."

Ellis laughed. "You don't look like you've ever had an ounce of weight on you. You're just as thin as you were in high school."

She snorted in response. "Just picture a walrus trying to flop from the ocean to his rock. That's what I looked like trying to get out of bed on my own."

"If I have it my way, you won't have to get out of bed on your own again." Ellis' dark eyes flashed. His hand brushed her exposed knee under the table.

Lizzie's stomach did the now familiar flip and tumble. "Wanna get out of here? Take the dessert to go?"

"I'm okay with that." Ellis' gaze was hungry. His finger danced its way up her thigh.

"Hey!" A familiar idea popped into her mind. "Want to sing some karaoke? We can act stupid, like we did when we were teens. It'll be so fun!" She could picture Ellis with his shirt unbuttoned even more, sweat dripping from his temples as he serenaded her with a goofy love song.

"I've got other plans for this evening," he said. "Let's take that to-go dessert back to my place."

Karaoke-Singing Ellis was replaced by a vision of At-Home Ellis, the button-up now fully taken off. Lizzie's stomach didn't have butterflies anymore; it was a freaking airplane in there. She nodded, words failing her.

"Excellent." Ellis grinned as he waved over the waiter.

The drive back to his apartment was short. Ellis helped Lizzie out of the car, his fingertips sending a shock through her hand as he led her to the elevator. She wondered if they would start there as they did last time, but the thought was cut short when a boy and his dog joined them for the ride up.

The doors to the elevator swung open to reveal a black foyer, Ellis' apartment. Ellis wished the kid a good night before guiding Lizzie out into the darkness. The boy waved goodbye, and the doors slid shut behind them. A small flicker broke up the shadows, produced by a lighter Ellis was holding. She could make out his smile behind the flame, smooth and suave as ever as he walked around the room lighting tiny tea light candles he had placed on the tables. Lizzie's breath caught in her throat. There were rose petals everywhere. A million of them, tiny and soft and perfect, appearing as though they were floating in the soft amber light of the candles. He'd thought of everything.

Ellis' hand found its way to the small of her back. "There's a bathroom to your left. Do you need a moment?"

She nodded, stomach still dancing. Ellis turned to make his way to the kitchen, and she left to feel for the bathroom door through the thick mask of darkness.

Once inside, she fumbled for the light switch and

flipped it on. Her own reflection took her by surprise, staring back at her from a mirror that felt just a little too closely placed. Without intention, her fingers found their way to her hair, twisting in the kinky blonde curls that had escaped from her updo. She looked good. Beautiful, even. But her insides still twisted as she thought about what waited for her when she undressed.

Lizzie pulled one strap of her dress down, then the other. The dark fabric fell to the floor and pooled around her feet. Reflecting back at her in the mirror was the familiar body she had woken up to every day for ten years. She was thin, yes, but the skin was no longer tight and taut. It was marred and heavy, hanging about her thighs and belly. Her breasts didn't help the effect; even in the lacy red bra she had borrowed from Nora, they looked drooped and sad.

She couldn't see Ellis this way. Not after the last time he'd seen her naked. She'd been on the Prom Court then, young and vibrant and gorgeous. Now. . . now she was a mother.

And no one wanted to be with the mother.

The dancing in her stomach was starting to make her feel sick. She braced herself with two hands on the sink countertop. She could hear Ellis out in the kitchen, popping a cork for something bubbly. Lizzie turned on the sink and splashed some of the cool water on her neck and chest. Her breathing was only intensifying. She couldn't slow the pace. Making up her mind, she reached down to pull up her dress, replacing the straps on her shoulders one by one. She left herself out of the bathroom and was greeted by Ellis, who held two glasses of sparkling gold.

"I didn't expect you to still be clothed," he said, his white teeth gleaming in the soft light. "But I can work with that."

Lizzie put a hesitant hand on his chest. "Ellis..."

His face soured. "Well, that's never a good start."

"I don't think I'm ready," she said, her voice as apologetic as she could muster. "We've only been out three times. Can't we take it a little slower? When I'm more comfortable—"

"We have taken it slow," he said. His voice was low and quiet. He set the glasses on a side table and stepped toward her. "We've waited for over ten years."

"That's not quite what I mean," Lizzie answered, blushing. She took a step back, too nervous to touch him again. "I just don't think that I'm ready this time."

His hands were on her waist, taking her by surprise. He pulled her close, his kisses landing hot and fast on her neck. "I want you now," he said. "I'm so enamored with you, Lizzie."

He started for the strap on her dress, and she quickly stopped his hand with hers. She could still see the image of her pale white body in the bathroom mirror. "Next time."

Ellis reached around the back of her dress, ripping the fabric open in one quick tear. "Oops," he grinned and stepped back, taking in the sight of her.

She couldn't look at him. "Ellis, no."

But to her surprise, he liked what he saw. He got down on his knees, kissing his way up her long, thin legs. A sound escaped her throat, carnal and wild.

"I think you mean yes," he said, chuckling.

She couldn't stop him. She was paralyzed, frozen by some unseen force that started in her chest and radiated out to her fingertips and toes. The protests still came to her lips, and she felt them as keenly as she had in the hallway, but he silenced them with kisses. He was dominating, sure, and quick.

The rest of the night went by in a blur. When it was over,

Ellis laid on her chest like a child, the sounds of his breathing steady and relaxed.

Lizzie was on her back, staring up at a ceiling too dark to see. And the memory she had been trying to forget for weeks came flooding back all at once.

They had gone to prom together. Of course they had. They were the perfect couple. Ellis and Elizabeth: destined to be together forever. He had bought her a corsage. She had bought him a boutonniere. And just like the night at Valentino's, there were expectations. He hadn't bothered getting a room back then. He had only taken her to his car, but she'd been just as thrilled. It had started hot and heavy, and she had thought that she was ready.

But she wasn't. And when she told him ...

She could still picture her corsage on the floor of his car, the petals trampled and dirty. She had wanted this, he assured her. She'd been talking about it for weeks. They had made plans. It was supposed to happen.

He had ripped her dress, the one that had cost her two weeks' paychecks. It was an exercise of passion, intended to seem romantic rather than dominating. But Lizzie had felt the same way as she did in his apartment: paralyzed, turned to stone. She repeated the same objections. She felt the same tears spill down her cheeks.

That's when David had thrown open the door. He'd pulled Ellis from the car, stopping him before he did what could not be undone. It had seemed unreal that he could handle the weight of such a heavy football player. He got in one good punch before Ellis was firing back, beating him until the side of his face was raw and red. Ellis had spat and run off, leaving David holding a shaking Lizzie in the parking lot before he took her back to his empty house, and the trajectory of their friendship had changed forever. Over the next few weeks, comfort turned to romance turned to something even deeper. Something that shook Lizzie just as much as prom night had, but in a very different way.

Lizzie worried that her quick breathing would wake Ellis, who slept on her chest. She concentrated to steady it, focusing in on a shadow she could just make out near the window.

I love you.

Ellis had said it just before he fell asleep. He'd nuzzled into her neck, kissing her deeply once more. Then he'd pulled back, run his thumb across her cheekbone, and said it. "I love you."

The tears ran down Lizzie's cheeks and she had to bite her lip to keep her choked sobs from waking him.

CHAPTER 17

"**W**E DID IT!" Clint ran into the girls' dressing room brandishing two noise-makers and wearing a party hat.

"Did you see my backflip?" Ashley popped her head through the door from behind him, her eyes wide with excitement.

"It was killer! And the closing—" Lizzie started.

"Magic!" Grace interjected, not bothering to wait for the door to close before she pulled her costume up and over her head. "Lord, openin' night could not have gone better. Praise Jesus!"

"Don't jinx us, we still have five more shows after tonight!" Ashley chided her optimism, but her own wide grin gave away her feelings.

"The crew is setting up for the after party out on the stage," Clint said.

"Save me something caffeinated?" Lizzie asked.

"You betcha!" He winked and disappeared with Ashley. Lizzie could hear them hooting and hollering all over again as they opened the second girls' dressing room down the hall.

"How am I supposed to sleep after a show like that?" The young girl next to Lizzie moaned. "I'll be up thinking it over all night!"

"It's over and done with, sweetheart." Grace walked over and put an arm around the girl's shoulders. "Now come party! Lizzie? You comin'?"

Lizzie pulled her hoodie over her head and slipped on the house slippers she'd brought for backstage. "You bet."

The gaggle of girls made their way through the dimly lit wings to the stage. It was decked to the nines in streamers and glitter, with a loaded-up snack table sitting square in the middle of the action. There was a happy murmur in the room as cast mates excitedly compared notes and swapped backstage stories. Lizzie spied David standing near the front of the stage with the actors who played Tevya and Lazar Wolf. He caught her eye and smiled, raising his drink in her direction. *Great show*, he mouthed.

Lizzie's phone went off in her pocket, making her jump. She pulled it out. *Ellis*. Her stomach clenched. She hadn't spoken to him since their night together. She hadn't wanted to. Before, she had thought that she was so grown up, so changed. That she could appreciate his surety. His passion.

His aggression.

Now, she knew it for what it was. And the thought of the night they had spent together made her sick. She pressed *ignore* on the call, placing the phone back in her pocket. It was already buzzing again by the time she pulled her hand away. She sighed, trying to brace herself. She stepped into the wings, answering the call.

"Ellis?"

"Lizzie!" His voice was light and breezy. It took her off

guard. "I'm out in the lobby. Is it ok if I come in? I can hear the party."

"What?"

"You left your wallet at my house. I was in the area and figured I'd bring it over after your show."

She didn't want to see him. She was transported in time, feeling like a teenager again. A teenager who didn't yet know she was pregnant, running to the other side of the country to get away from her ex-boyfriend. Her stomach lurched. She'd have to get it back from him sometime. *Be brave, Lizzie.*

"Yeah," she answered. "You can let yourself in. I'll come down and meet you."

The phone clicked off and Lizzie started toward the edge of the stage. She could see Ellis opening the doors from the lobby, his smile as broad and beaming as ever. She waved to get his attention.

"Hey, I'm over—" She was cut off by the sound of shattering glass. Lizzie turned to find Margo standing by the stage door, a punch bowl fractured into a million shining pieces laying at her feet. The woman was visibly shaking. Her mouth hung open as though frozen on words she could not say.

"Margo?" Ellis called as he hopped up onto the stage. His smile had widened. His white teeth gleamed. "I didn't know you were in this show, too. It's been a while."

Something clicked in Lizzie's brain.

David flew into action. He ran up to Ellis, pushing him back with both hands. "Get out of here!" He barked. "You're not welcome at the Baron."

"Relax, Flannery." Ellis smiled again and ran a hand through his coifed hair. "No need to get defensive. I'm just saying hi to an old friend. You know all about friendship, right?"

David pulled back his fist and punched Ellis square in the jaw, sending him tumbling off the stage. Margo was sobbing, the sounds loud and wailing even over the violence. Ellis pushed himself up to his feet, his hand rubbing his smarting jaw. His eyes flashed as he looked up to Lizzie. "Are you seriously going to let him act this way again? I thought you'd outgrown him." He took a menacing step in David's direction, hand clenched by his side.

"You're back together with him?" David looked back at Lizzie, the hurt in his eyes apparent even through the seething rage. He knew then. He could see it in her face what Ellis had tried once more. But this time ... this time David Flannery wasn't the soft boy he was in high school. And he wouldn't let Ellis off without paying for what he'd done. He jumped off the stage, pushing Ellis back once more. "Don't you dare come near her again."

Ellis threw his own punch to the stomach, but David side-stepped the blow. He beat Ellis down to the ground, his fists pounding over and over and over again. Lizzie could hear more screaming, but she realized this time that it wasn't just coming from Margo. It was coming from her.

Finally, Ellis scrambled to his feet. His nose was bleeding, and the skin was already mottling. "You'll pay for that, Flannery. Expect a call from my father." He pulled Lizzie's wallet from his pocket, throwing it on the floor and spitting on it. "Here, bitch. Don't try to contact me ever again."

"You won't have to worry about that," David snarled, pushing him back toward the lobby doors. When Ellis was gone, David turned and sprinted back to the stage. He pushed himself up and ran over to the girls. On the floor, Lizzie held Margo in her arms as tight as she could to stop the shaking. David got down on the floor with them, holding them both tight before bending down to offer Margo his cardigan. "You can wipe your face with this," he said. "God, Mar, I'm so sorry."

"You should be," Lizzie said. David looked up at her, clearly surprised. The words had surprised her, too, but once they started coming, she found that she couldn't stop them. "What are you, a Neanderthal? You punch a guy out in your own theater and embarrass Margo even further?"

David's eyes were fire. "I was *protecting you*, Lizzie. Protecting you both. He's a predator—"

"I don't need your protection," Lizzie spat back. "I never have."

"Geez, Hancock, did you get a head injury back in Jersey? Do you not remember what he tried to do to you on prom night? I'm not letting him near another person I care about ever again."

Margo looked up at Lizzie with wide eyes. "Ellis hurt you, too?"

"I'm not your best friend from high school anymore, David!" She could see in his face how the words stung him, but she pushed on. "I've changed. And if there's one thing I've learned, it's that I have to live with the consequences of my own choices. You don't get a second chance and you don't get a do-over. There's no amount of punching and kicking on your part that's going to change that for me. I don't need you."

Saying the words out loud made her feel ill. They were her leaving town after graduation and never calling David again. They were audition after audition in New York, with no success. They were a positive pregnancy test and not having the guts to reach out to the father. They were her unspoken betrayal, finally given voice. She truly believed it;

life didn't give out second chances. And it was suddenly clear to her that returning to Warner Robins had been a part of an elaborate fantasy.

Maybe this reaction was childish and impulsive. Maybe she'd regret it in a few days or even in a few minutes. But Lizzie refused to think about that. She just wanted to get out of the Baron and stop thinking about the monumental list of mistakes she'd made and faults she possessed.

She stood up, brushing off her jeans. David reached for her arm, but she shrugged him off. She knew that the rest of the cast was watching, too embarrassed by proxy to interrupt her grand exit. She pretended that they weren't there, but nonetheless desperately willed back the tears she felt stinging at her eyes. She snatched up her wallet from where Ellis had thrown it and grabbed her bag, barreling out of the exit and leaving the Baron, doors swinging behind her, intending not to make the mistake of coming back again.

CHAPTER 18

*L*izzie was far from present on her drive home from the theater. It was a miracle that she made it to the house in one piece, not having recognized at all which turns she was making or for which lights she was stopping or going. Her tears had obscured her vision, running messy tracks down her face and through her heavy stage makeup.

She knew by then that she shouldn't have yelled at David. The regret stung deep in her chest. It was a feeling she was becoming all too familiar with experiencing. Still, the conversation was one she'd been having in her head for close to ten years. Those were the words that had kept her in New Jersey, the words that had stopped her from trying so many things. They'd come rushing forth now, not because it was the appropriate time or place, but, rather, because they could not be suppressed for any longer.

When Lizzie arrived at the Grant-Thornton house, she took a moment to sit in the car and attempt to clean her face. Her sleeves quickly turned black and brown with the muddied stage makeup. She knew that her tears would be apparent despite her best efforts. Yet again, here was something she'd mucked up that was now seemingly beyond her control. She sighed and let herself out of the car.

The deck door was locked. She knocked, her impatience turning into a headache. No answer. She knocked again, louder. She heard something crash in the house. She fished the house key Nora had given her out of her purse, fumbling with the lock until it clicked in her hand. Another crash came as she opened the door, followed by a loud sob.

"Nora, please let us help you."

The kitchen was chaos. Bill stood at the stovetop, waving a rag at the black smoke that puffed out from a burning pot of okra. Young Caroline was sitting at the table, her head thrown back into a wail as she clutched at the pieces of a broken glass. Nora stood in the center of the room with Poppy, her hands locked tight around his elbows. Her eyes were big and wide with worry.

"She's hurt herself this time; I just know it." Nora shook him. Her own tears were running wet streaks down her cheeks. "We have to go look for her! You're a doctor for goodness' sake!"

"You're scaring the child," Poppy admonished. His face was twisted with his own worry. He took Nora by the chin, looking deep into her eyes. "You have to snap out of this one, baby."

"You unfeeling bastard!" Nora's voice escalated into a scream. "She could be passed out somewhere. Her meds could be wrong. What if she had a spell in the car again? You have to do *something!*"

Nora spotted Lizzie standing in the doorway and rushed over to her. The fire alarm began to squeal and Caroline wailed louder. "Quiet!" Nora hissed at her. She grabbed Lizzie by the arm and started toward the door. "Liz, Ma's gone again. I just know something happened to her. We have to go find her—"

"Your mom?" Lizzie shook her head, confused. "Nora, your mom—"

The alarm finally relented as Bill slapped at it with his towel. Poppy rushed up to the women, grabbing Nora's hand. "We can go looking in my car," he offered. "We can see if she's still at work down at the high school? Or maybe she went to my office. There's no need to panic yet."

Nora struggled to steady her breathing through her tears. "Good idea. Lizzie, can you check by the hospital? I worry she's hurt."

Lizzie nodded, swallowing down a thick lump that had formed in her throat. "Of course. I'll be right behind you."

"Bill, can you stay here if Ma comes home? I know you're not supposed to be here after ten, but we can make an exception, right?" Nora looked to her father, who nodded.

"Let's hurry along now," he said, urging her out the door. "We don't want Ma to get cold out there."

"Oh God ..." Fresh tears sprang from Nora's eyes as she pulled open the door and rushed out with Poppy.

Their departure left the kitchen feeling eerie and oddly deflated. Smoke still hung thick in the air, and Caroline continued to sniffle and moan despite Bill's best efforts to calm her. Finally, he gave her a tight squeeze and sent her out to the hallway.

"Why don't you go find the other kids upstairs?" he asked. "They probably need someone brave like you around."

Bill turned to Lizzie, placing the smoke-blackened rag over his shoulder. He looked impossibly tired. His shoulders sagged under some unseen weight. "She didn't want you to find out this way. She'd been doing so well lately."

Lizzie put a hand to her forehead, willing her headache to subside. She collapsed into the chair Caroline had been using at the kitchen table. "Is she—"

"Early onset Alzheimer's," he confirmed, his voice clearly struggling to form the words aloud. "Very early. We got the diagnosis back in March." He sat down beside her, rubbing his own temples. Lizzie could see now the age on his face that she hadn't been able to see before. "It started with little things. Her work keys would magically go missing. She forgot about Mary-Kate's birthday cake. Episodes like these don't come along very often." He laughed. The sound felt strange and obtrusive in Lizzie's ears. "She called me at work the other day and asked me about Trig homework. Can you believe that?" He rubbed at his eyes with his palms, still laughing dryly.

"She thinks her Ma is missing again?"

"It's always that night when the episodes get really bad. She's reliving finding her collapsed by the high school."

"That's awful." She could feel the tears stinging at her eyes once more.

"It's the worst night of her life happening over and over and over again." Bill shook his head. He collapsed into his hands, the sobs coming without shame.

"I'm a fool." Lizzie closed her eyes, rubbing a spot on the bridge of her nose. "I should have guessed. But I was so freaking caught up in my own problems. The theater. David. Ellis. Oh God, Ellis..."

Bill shook his head. "She worked hard to make sure you wouldn't guess until she could tell you herself."

"That's why I'm here, isn't it?" She didn't bother to form the words as a question. "I'm not the kids' nanny. I'm hers."

"I'm not sure that's how she'd like you to put it," Bill's mouth turned up into a grim imitation of a smile. "But yes.

We needed someone to make sure that the house still ran. That she was taken care of. But that wasn't the only reason you're here."

Lizzie laughed, the dry sound surprising her. "She's meddling then."

"Nora never did like to leave an end untied. And if you were going to take care of her, then she was going to take care of you." Bill reached out to hold her hand. "This is your home now, Lizzie. She wants it that way. But more than that, she wants to give you a second chance."

Lizzie sighed. "I think it's too late for that. And besides, lately I'm not so sure I believe in second chances." She massaged the bridge of her nose once more. "I really screwed this up."

He squeezed her hand again. Lizzie's chest felt like it was frozen. She struggled to breathe, struggled to think straight.

Her best friend—the beautiful, ambitious, smart young doctor who was going to change the world—was just as stuck in the past as Lizzie was. She was reliving the worst part of her life, suspended between what could be and what was. And there was no going back.

There was no cure for Alzheimer's, that much was common knowledge. Nora would only get worse as time went on. She'd forget her children. She'd forget Bill and Poppy. She'd forget every beautiful thing that had ever made her happy. It was a half-life, at best.

And reliving the past wasn't any way to live at all. Better to go always forward, never back.

Lizzie had a vision of Nora on the back deck then, standing under a steel gray Georgia sky as she smoked one last cigarette.

It's ancient history, her friend was telling her. *But it still happened. We still happened. Warner Robins is part of you. You can't ignore that.*

There was a tumbling sound of hurried feet on the stairs. Mary-Kate appeared in the doorway, followed by a very worried-looking Hazel.

"Dad, he left."

"What?" Bill asked. "Who, baby? Poppy?"

"Fullmer," Mary-Kate explained.

Hazel stepped forward, her eyes pleading with her mother. "I tried to stop him, Mom. I told him not to get all freaked out like he does. But when Nora started screaming, he started crying and pacing and counting everything. The next thing I know, he's climbing out of our window and down the side of the house."

"*What?*" Lizzie shot out of her seat. "Did he say where he was going?"

Hazel started to cry. "He said he didn't want to leave Warner Robins. He thought that Nora was tired of us being here."

Lizzie knelt down on Hazel's level and held her daughter by the shoulders. "Focus! Do you have any ideas where he might be?"

Hazel just cried harder in response. Lizzie hugged her tight and looked up to Bill. "Can I borrow the car again?"

"It's yours," he nodded. "I'll get the kids to bed."

"Thanks," she said. She pulled on her coat and headed toward the backdoor.

Outside, the clouds were pressing down even harder than before, suffocating Lizzie as she made her way back to the car. She zipped her coat all the way up and crossed her arms to fight back the chill that threatened to seep into her clothing.

After a drive that felt like an eternity, she had tried all

the spots she could imagine. He wasn't walking the neighborhood streets as she might have hoped. He'd made it out of the community, and Lizzie worried about the busy road that waited beyond the HOA gates. She tried the elementary school next. No luck there, either. She thought of the library. The music store. Fullmer was nowhere to be seen. Suddenly she was all too aware of the terror Nora must feel as she combed the streets for a mother that had died by the high school over half a decade ago.

Sometime after midnight, Lizzie returned to the Grant-Thornton house, beaten down and anxious as ever. Poppy's beaten old Chevy was parked off by the pine trees, and Lizzie considered asking him to take his own route now that Nora had presumably been returned to bed. She quickly got out of the car, leaving the engine still running.

Lights swept up the house. Lizzie turned and shielded her eyes as a car turned into the drive behind her. It parked, the lights switching off. David Flannery got out of the driver's seat.

"David." The knot in her stomach twisted tighter. She sighed and waved him off. "Go home. I don't have time right now."

"I know," he answered, opening his back door. He bent over and reached in, emerging with a small form in his arms. Fullmer's head flopped to the side of his arm, his glasses sliding down the length of his nose as he snored softly. He was wrapped in one of David's oversized cardigans.

"Oh my God!" Lizzie rushed over, scooping her son into her own arms and hugging him tight. This time her tears surprised her, springing out so fast she had no time to wipe them away.

"Mom?" Fullmer looked confused and groggy as he raised his head to look at his mother.

She set him on the ground and patted his back. "Head inside, love," she said. "Bill should be waiting to help you get to bed."

The young boy staggered off to the house, still rubbing his tired eyes with confusion. Lizzie turned back to David. She crossed her arms and shook her head. "David, I—"

"He showed up at the theater a while after you left," David explained. "Lucky I still had a lot to do with opening night. He only had on a pajama t-shirt and shorts when he was waiting at my front door."

"Why did he come to you?"

"He likes me," David shrugged. He wouldn't look up at her. Instead, he watched his feet and kicked at a rock in the driveway. "He said he was scared that you were going to get kicked out and have to head back to Jersey. He wanted to stay with me. So I gave him some crackers and sparkling cider, and we chatted for a while. I think he's okay now."

"David ..." Lizzie didn't know what to say. She felt like the world had started spinning around her. The words she had thrown at him back at the theater came bubbling up in her mind, popping off like fireworks that branded her brain. Here he was, rescuing her again. She hadn't given him a second chance, but he had found one, anyway. And to her surprise, she felt grateful. Beyond grateful. "Why did you do this for me after everything I said to you?"

"Geez, Lizzie, your expectations for men are incredibly low." He laughed a little and finally looked up from his shoes. "You're important to me. You're never going to stop being important to me. There's nothing you can say or do that's going to change that. Try all you want."

His green eyes gleamed in the soft moonlight. They were

the color of kudzu, Lizzie thought. The color of something foreign and wild and beautiful that insisted upon being noticed. Something that had nestled into the heart of Georgia and made its home, as natural a fit to the landscape as the red clay or the delicate honeysuckle.

She was pulling him toward her then, kissing his mouth and relishing the sweet taste of cider from his post-show drink. His hands found their way to the small of her back, where they drew her closer. She could feel the quick and steady beat of his heart on her chest.

Suddenly, he was pulling back, a thumb on the lips she had just been kissing. "Lizzie," he shook his head, his eyes pained.

"Oh God." Embarrassment flushed her cheeks and made her feel numb. "I'm so sorry."

"No," David tried to take her hand, but she pulled it away. "I just don't want it to be this way. I—"

"You don't have to explain," she said quickly, pulling her coat tight around her body as she started back toward the house. "Thank you for bringing Fullmer home," she called over her shoulder. She didn't turn back to see if he was leaving, too.

CHAPTER 19

"*I* wish you'd stay." Nora sat on the edge of Lizzie's bed, her face downcast and her hands folded conservatively in her lap.

Lizzie sighed and sat down next to her on the comforter. She put an arm around her old friend, squeezing her shoulders. "This is what Ashley does for a living, Nor. She'll be about a hundred thousand times better at it than your untrained, diner waitress best friend."

The arrangements had been surprisingly easy to make. Lizzie had called up Ashley, who worked for an in-home care company. She seemed like a perfect fit: young and kind, but experienced and—more importantly—fully equipped to deal with Nora's unique circumstances. She would come to the house every day, checking in on the family as Nora started to transition her practice over to her partners.

While the plans had been simple, the conversation surrounding Lizzie's departure had not. Nora had a good humor about her diagnosis, but no amount of jokes or jabs could erase the clear pain and uncertainty that accompanied the beginnings of Alzheimer's at such a young age. In the end, she had pleaded with Lizzie to change her mind. The money would be good, she promised. The kids had a home here. Everyone loved them.

But Lizzie's mind was made up. Despite the realization that coming to Warner Robins might not have been the worst thing for her, she still felt like a huge idiot for kissing David only to be rejected. Clearly, she had gotten her second chance with him and mucked it up by acting like a jerk when Ellis showed up at the theater. She was embarrassed and eager to put it all behind her.

She could try to get her job back at another diner in another far-off city, she thought. Far, far away from where David Flannery could run into her and remember how flip-floppy she'd acted or how immature she'd been when he came to her defense. Lizzie was more than aware that this was likely how David had felt when she had rejected him and run off to New Jersey after graduation, a fact that sent a stab into her chest every time it popped into her brain. He must have felt just as humiliated.

But back to the business at hand. Nora could get better care than Lizzie could ever give her, and they'd already had the best goodbye they could ask for. Hazel would adjust to another new school, no problem. And Fullmer... Well, maybe it was time to invest in a second-hand saxophone. He could play at home and be happy there. Warner Robins was no longer strictly off limits, but Lizzie's time spent there could at the very least be relegated to short visits at Nora's house.

David had called her over and over again. The first time she didn't show up for a performance, she had to tuck her cell phone under a pillow to ignore his voicemails. She had sat on the carpet twisting her hair around her finger, praying to every ancient God she could think of that her stomach would stop spinning in circles. She wanted to get out of the city fast and put as much distance between her and the Baron as possible. Closing night was coming up that night, and she didn't even want to think about it.

"They tell me that, when I have an episode, recognizing familiar faces helps to keep me grounded in reality." Nora's voice was soft. "I never did know Ashley Walker too well."

"You can get to know her." Lizzie leaned over and kissed her friend's cheek. "The new memories you make will be great ones."

"Isn't there anything I can say or do to convince you to stay? Do I have to start foaming at the mouth or something?"

Lizzie laughed. "I'll visit."

"You've said that before."

"This time I mean it," Lizzie promised. She got up and pulled her loaded suitcase out from under the bed. "Now can you help me get this thing downstairs for tomorrow? I'm not sure why I ever bothered having two kids if neither one will help me with the heavy lifting."

Nora managed a small smile. "Sure, ask the invalid."

"Buck up, buckaroo." Lizzie grinned at her. They both grabbed an end of the suitcase and took the stairs together. Lizzie waved Nora off to the living room. "Go lie down now. I'm fine the rest of the way to the car."

The wheels ran heavy and loud over the hardwood until Lizzie reached the kitchen linoleum. She squeezed her bag through the narrow door and walked it over to the back of the car. She popped the trunk and grunted as she heaved the bag up and over the edge into its resting place. She sighed. This was barely a dent in what she needed to have packed by the morning.

The sound of music drifted over to her. She turned to

see Poppy on the back deck, Fullmer standing dutifully by his side. Poppy was pointing out at the woods behind the house. Fullmer's face was messy with tears, but a smile was showing through anyway as he got excited about whatever was off in the distance. Lizzie closed the trunk and walked over to join them.

"You're just in time," Poppy said, pulling her over and slipping his arm around her shoulders. "Fullmer just found a deer out in the grass."

"Poppy found it," Fullmer corrected, blushing. "Look! It has a friend!"

"So it does." Lizzie smiled and pulled her son close to join their huddle.

"That's a baby," Poppy noted. "See the white spots?" As if on cue, the little fawn turned to the glow of the deck light, showing off its patchwork of white spots. "The marks are a kind of camouflage. They help the deer hide from predators. They lose the spots when they get older. Don't need 'em anymore."

"Deer must be pretty brave," Fullmer commented.

"Must you really deprive your child of the spectacular beauty that is Georgia nature?" Poppy turned to Lizzie, elbowing her in the side and winking. "Last I checked, New Jersey doesn't have lightnin' bug season in the summer or cotton fields in the early fall."

"I want to see a lightning bug, Mom!" Fullmer's uncontrollable eagerness lit up his face.

"Maybe we'll come back for a visit then," she said, squeezing him tight. "Let's just enjoy one more perfect night here for now. You've got the lighting, the scenery, the music... I like this song, I think. What is it again, Fullmer?"

The record player spun happily on the table behind them. The music was chaotic and unpredictable, with notes that jumped out of nowhere and rang out like ancient heralds. Lizzie found her foot tapping. She let the bare hint of a beat shimmy up through her body, guiding her to dance and sway. She took Fullmer's hands and twirled him around. When he whipped back in front of her, his eyes were wide with excitement.

"It's the Coltrane stuff. David fixed my record player, remember?"

The music swelled, and Lizzie swayed her hips. "This is the best part."

"You have a favorite part? I thought jazz was all a jumbled mess to you, Mom. It gave you a headache."

Lizzie stopped dancing. "... You're right. I don't remember it making any real sense before now."

Poppy raised an eyebrow and offered her his own hand. She took it and he pulled her to his chest, swaying her back and forth to the beat. "So just to get this straight—" he twirled her "—what didn't make sense to you before magically does after a trip back home? Darlin', you can't ignore somethin' like that."

She stopped him with a hand to his chest. She turned away from them both, knowing that the pink rising in her cheeks would give away her feelings. "We're leaving, Poppy. That's that."

"Quit running, child. Live in the blissfully unexpected here and now."

"We can't go yet, Mom." Fullmer chimed in. His voice was low and quiet, and Lizzie thought to herself that he looked just about as grown up as he ever had. "We need to be here."

She got down on her knees and brushed the hair from his bright little eyes. "Aunt Nora will have a nurse, buddy.

And Hazel and you will get a cool, new school and we'll visit here during breaks and—"

"But if we leave, we'll never see my dad again. And I was starting to really like him."

Lizzie was taken aback. She stood up, feeling a bit dizzy. "...How long have you known?"

"You always say that you didn't raise us to be dumb." Fullmer grinned up at her.

"'Mer..." There were a thousand things she had planned on saying to her son about his dad when the time was right. They all escaped her. "He doesn't know yet. I was too scared to tell him. I ran away when things got serious. I made my choice ten years ago and to renege on it now just because I'm feeling a little swept up and some godforsaken jazz music starts making sense... that feels..."

"You're runnin' out of excuses, child." Poppy laughed.

Lizzie ran a hand through her hair. "I don't know what to do."

"Well," Poppy reached into his pocket and produced a white slip of paper. His face was pure mischief. "Lucky for you, I already bought your tickets."

"For *Fiddler*? I can't show my face around there. I can't even think about looking at him—"

"Mom," Fullmer interrupted. He put a hand on his hip. "Poppy didn't raise you to be dumb."

CHAPTER 20

"*A*re you sure you're up for this today?"

Lizzie sat with Margo in the car they'd borrowed from Nora. They held hands over the center console, their fingers intertwined like neither would make it if they broke apart.

It had taken a lot of guts for Lizzie to call up Margo. After she'd gone inside from her time on the deck with Poppy and Fullmer, she'd dialed and hung up at least three times before actually making the call. Every instinct told her to go finish packing, to run off and forget about everything in Warner Robins once more.

But she knew now that she couldn't do that. Her darn son had outsmarted her.

She was going to have to wrap up some loose ends, even if it meant sticking around in town for a little longer. And if she was going to start in on loose ends, then she had to take care of the biggest thing first.

She had to face up to what had happened with Ellis.

Lizzie nodded to Margo. "If I don't do this now, I never

will. I went a decade in silence before. It could happen again."

Margo squeezed her fingers and turned in her seat to look at Lizzie. Her eyes had gone large and round. They welled up with tears that threatened to spill out onto her cheeks. "I know that I said I regret not reporting, but this is your choice to live with Lizzie. This is a big deal."

The words didn't really need to be spoken, but Lizzie felt their full impact anyway: it *was* a big deal. A massive deal. Life-changing, even. Once she reported Ellis and his sexual assault on her to the police, it couldn't be undone.

Because that's what it was, she reminded herself: a sexual assault. She had said no, but he had said yes.

Politics didn't matter. The way that her friends and classmates and old neighbors would react didn't matter. In the end, Ellis had taken something from Lizzie that hadn't been his to take. He'd done the same thing to Margo, and presumably to other women before them. He couldn't keep getting away with it, or he would keep doing it. And other women would find themselves in the same parking spot that Margo and Lizzie waited in now, staring up at the formidable police station and feeling like they might throw up at the prospect of having to relive the worst days of their lives.

Giving it a name still hadn't made her experience feel quite real. This kind of thing happened to people on TV, not to Lizzie. But when she'd first called Margo, and they'd talked it over and Margo had used the words "sexual assault," Lizzie knew that she couldn't just pretend like her situation wasn't real. Ellis Clarke was no better than Kavinsky at the Starshine Diner: he had a prettier face and a smoother operation, sure, but he was just as guilty. Lizzie couldn't ignore it all over again and live in ignorance. Something had to be done, even if it did mean having to stay in Warner Robins a little longer than she had anticipated. Even if it meant that, in the process, she'd feel just as exposed as Ellis.

Even if it meant having to tell David the truth. The whole truth.

Lizzie wasn't naïve. She knew that there likely wasn't much that could be done about what happened to her. She had made no secret of her pursuit of Ellis Clarke. She'd worn all the pretty dresses, been to all the nice restaurants. She'd gossiped with her girlfriends and even hoped for a kiss at the end of a date night. All of the signs that she "wanted him" were in place for cops, lawyers, or a jury to see. There was no evidence to be held against Ellis. There was a very strong possibility that nothing would ever take him down legally.

But in the same intimate, deeply personal way that Lizzie understood her own role in what had happened to her, she understood how Warner Robins worked. It was a small town. People talked.

She cleared her throat and squeezed Margo's hand back. "For years, I was absolutely horrified at the prospect of what people would think of me if I returned to my hometown. I predicted the multitude of ways that I could be judged. I had recurring nightmares about what could be said behind my back. All that fear, and I hadn't even done anything wrong. I had committed no crime except for failing to live up to my own expectations."

Lizzie shifted in her seat. She pulled Margo's hand to her chest and let her feel the steady beating of her heart. She didn't know what waited for them inside the police station, but she was going to gather the courage to enter.

"If I can live through fear like that," Lizzie started. "Then certainly Ellis Clarke can survive his own dose of it. Let him be the one who fears his neighbors' judgements. Let his clients question his integrity. Let his coworkers wonder about the dates he goes on over the weekend. Let him be the one who has the nightmares, for once."

Margo nodded. She looked like there were a million things that she wanted to say, all waiting behind her lips at once. But she settled for pulling Lizzie's hand to her mouth and delicately kissing the curves of her fingers. "Thank you," she whispered.

Lizzie nodded and grabbed the handle of the car door.

The voicemails started coming in before Lizzie had even made it back to Nora's house.

I'm going to kill that guy!

Lizzie, I'm so sorry, I just heard...

Seriously? Ellis Clarke?

So much for anonymity.

But Lizzie had known this was coming. She had braced for it even, listening to soft, sweet 70s rock with Margo the whole drive back to drop her off, willing herself into a place of peace.

As she'd always known, Warner Robins was small, and the gossip got around fast. The cop who took her statement must have told his colleagues, and from there the news had burst forth and turned into its own beast. Wives would have been the first to know. Neighbors next, maybe. Teenage children. Lizzie supposed that by the next morning there wouldn't be a person in town who wouldn't know all the intimate details of her report.

It was a terrifying feeling, even seeing messages of support. Her big secret—that clandestine part of herself that even she had been afraid to poke at for over a decade—had finally found new life. It was beyond her grasp now. She couldn't bottle it up again, even if she tried.

Even worse, though, was the feeling she got when she started seeing the less-than-supportive messages come through. Old friends from high school that she hadn't realized still had her number were writing to let her know that she must have misconstrued the situation. A cast member from *Fiddler* reached out to tell her that she had been on a date with Ellis Clarke once, and everything that happened between them was consensual. When Lizzie finally got a text from Ellis himself, she turned off her phone for good, not intending to read its messages until she was in a much better place.

Margo had prepared her for this. It was a horror story, the kind of tale that Lizzie had kept herself from thinking about for a very long time before now. Margo told her how she'd lost friends when she first started coming out with the truth. She told her how her own mother had asked what she had been wearing on her date that night, as if there were some way that she had tempted Ellis into doing what he'd done. It had been a torture that didn't relent through waking or sleeping; Margo had been plagued with nightmares for years that even therapy hadn't done a whole lot to rid her of.

Lizzie had thought she was prepared. She thought she was in a strong enough place to handle the pressure, far enough removed from her old life in Warner Robins to not take the attacks personally. But the messages she got regarding her report were already putting her to the test.

Finally, she made it back to Nora's house. She hadn't told anyone that she was going with Margo to the police station, so no one was home to greet her. Her kids' little suitcases were packed and waiting by the front door. Lizzie wondered if maybe Poppy had taken the group out for ice cream or something. One final hurrah before the big goodbye.

What would she tell her children when they found out

the news? She had never considered that part before. Lizzie reached out to Hazel's pink suitcase, where her daughter had tied a fluffy yellow pompom around the handle. Fullmer's luggage had dinosaurs on the side. They were just babies.

Lizzie's stomach wrenched when she considered what she might say to explain this to her best friend, too. She had always told Nora everything, even when the truth stung. But Ellis had been her one holdout. She'd tried harder to imagine that nothing untoward had happened between them rather than tell her best friend the intimate details of what had really happened. For crying out loud, Nora had helped Lizzie to pick out date night outfits and gushed over the flowers that Ellis had brought her. Had Lizzie unintentionally made her friend look like a fool?

And then something even worse occurred to her. Nora's memory was changing. It was sand through a sieve, slipping away faster than Lizzie had ever realized. Would she have to retell the story of her assault over and over again, reliving its painful details each time she wanted to confide in her old friend?

You can do this. She reaffirmed her decision once more. She would find a way to talk to them. She would find a way to bring closure to all of this. She had to.

Lizzie took a deep breath and started up the stairs. After all, she had a show to get ready for. She felt a little dizzy at the thought of another confrontation in one day. Did she really have it in her to do this?

She opened her bedroom door. Her eyes immediately fell on the gorgeous green dress that Nora had laid out on the bedspread for her. It was more modest than the previous gowns that Nora had lent her. It had long, three-quarter length sleeves and a hemline that would hit mid-calf. She loved it instantly.

Lizzie closed her door and began to change. She pulled the green dress over her head and smoothed it down to fit the curves of her body. She stepped over to the old dresser mirror, sizing herself up as she fixed her hair.

And there it was: the familiar body she'd seen a million times stared back at her. But this time, she liked what she saw. Her shoulders were strong and proud. Her hips full and round from the privilege of months spent carrying her children. Her eyes were fierce and her smile genuine.

You can do this. Once more, the mantra repeated. This time, she really believed it.

CHAPTER 21

*L*izzie could hardly recognize the Baron as she saw it then. It was her first time in years attending as a patron rather than a performer, and the building looked transformed in its glow up for show night.

She slipped in the lobby doors behind a young family clad in heavy coats and hats, their cheeks rosy with both the chill and the excitement. The room was packed with other audience members. They were bathed in the soft, amber glow of the chandelier. The lights twinkled merrily off martini glasses from the bar and wristwatches being checked with anticipation as the time neared for the show to open. The lobby's red velvet walls and brass details were relics from another time, transporting the waiting audience into the golden age of theater. With the instrumental score of *Fiddler* playing on the overhead speakers, Lizzie could have sworn that she was back in New York City. She hung off to a side, flipping up her collar so she wouldn't be recognized by an usher.

When the time came to find her seat, she slipped in without grabbing a program. She found her number at the edge of a row and pulled off her own coat before she sat down. It was an odd feeling, sitting and waiting. She was so used to being on the other side of things now, and a pang of guilt swept through her chest as she thought about what her fellow actors were doing to prepare backstage. She regretted not getting the program now.

"Excuse me?" She tapped a young mother down the row. "Could I borrow that for a moment?"

The woman slipped her their program and Lizzie flipped to the cast page. The insert she was looking for slipped out before she found the right page. *Tonight, Golde will be played by Margo Robinson. Thank you.*

The lights flashed, warning the audience to quiet down and prepare for the show. The steady buzz simmered into nothingness as the lights retreated into full blackness. A spotlight shone on center stage. The audience clapped as David walked on, his trademark cardigan replaced by a maroon blazer over his black turtleneck. His beard had been trimmed, she noticed. His hair carefully brushed back. He smiled at the patrons and waved a hand.

Lizzie sunk down into her chair a bit further. He would know about her report by now, wouldn't he?

"Welcome to the Baron Theater!" The audience cheered and David's grin expanded. He waved again. "Thank you, thank you. We're excited to share our production of *Fiddler on the Roof* with all of you. Please turn off your cell phones and remain quiet for the duration of the show. There will be a brief intermission after Act I. Now, enjoy! *To life!*"

"*L'chaim!*" Someone from the audience called back. A ripple of laughter went through the crowd as certain patrons recognized the quote from the show. David smiled and waved again before heading offstage. The lights faded to black once more and Lizzie felt a rush of relief.

The strong fiddle of the first number cut through the darkness. The sound sent a spark through Lizzie's body. She couldn't help herself; she was smiling and tapping her fingers on the arm of her chair. When the lights cut on, the actor who played Tevya stood center stage.

His opening monologue introduced the tiny village of Anatevka, where every citizen was just trying to get by, just trying to survive and do the best that they could. Immediately, Lizzie was completely transported. She marveled at how good the show really was. The music was bright and crisp and clear, delivered with the kind of passion that only comes from those who can really relate to the Anatevka experience. Hints of the Southern accent rang through on the r's and g's, but they made the lyrics all the more endearing.

And the dancing! It had really come together. Men pulled off impressive leaps and lifts. Ashley nailed her backflip. The rush of bodies moved seamlessly in a whirl of colorful village costumes.

Margo was a joy filling in as Golde. Lizzie still felt the pang in her heart as she watched the part she had willingly abandoned, but she couldn't help but recognize the talent as she saw it. Part of her wondered why David hadn't asked Margo to play Golde in the first place. She gripped the arm of her chair tighter at the sudden memory of David standing just a few feet from where she sat now, avoiding eye contact with her as she sang her audition song. Perhaps she knew why he gave her the part after all.

Throughout each song, though, the words to that opening monologue kept ringing in her ears. It was a monologue that Lizzie had heard a thousand times in rehearsal, but it truly resonated now as she thought of all the people she had reconnected with in her own hometown. Bill and

Nora, piecing together what family life they could in the midst of tragedy. Margo, picking up the ruins of her life and learning how to trust again. David, rejected and heartbroken, but pressing on to build up his small, glorious kingdom at the Baron.

Maybe even Lizzie was a fiddler on the roof. Maybe it was time to give herself some credit for the life she had carved out for herself and her children. Her heart beat faster.

At the end of the first act, Lizzie overcame her anxieties and approached an usher about getting a program after all. Thankfully, the young, pimply teen didn't recognize her, and she took the folded slip of paper without incident. She returned to her seat and leafed through the pages, pouring over page after page of her co-stars' dedications to family and friends. Her pride for the cast pulled against her desire for anonymity.

Soon, the lights in the audience were dimming once more. The second act was somehow even better than the first. Margo sang "Do You Love Me?" to her Tevya with raw honesty, bringing stinging tears to Lizzie's eyes. Lizzie sang under breath with the show's final number, "Anatevka." When the curtain closed, she was the first to jump to her feet and applaud. The whole audience followed suit. She wolf-whistled, the sound making the children down the row from Lizzie giggle in delight.

The standing ovation continued through all the bows. Lizzie yelled out a cheer when Grace, Clint, and Ashley took a bow with the ensemble. She whistled again when Margo took her bow. The audience responded especially well to her performance, a rise in volume sweeping over the crowd. The actor who played Tevya took his bow. Then, the tech crew. Finally, David stepped out in front of the stage. He raised an arm and smiled. The house lights went up.

Lizzie couldn't help but feel a touch exposed in the sudden bright light. She let the rest of her row exit around her and she hung back, hoping to fade into the crowd as her castmates exited the stage to say hello to friends. David stayed at the front of the theater, overcome by a rush of elderly patrons who wanted to shake his hand. He looked so happy. She watched him from afar, a voyeur to the love and devotion his community clearly felt for him.

He'd directed an incredible show. He'd choreographed stellar numbers and brought out the best in his actors. He'd changed the face of the Baron, too, his hard labor showing through in its newly polished, professional look. It was always a wonderful theater. It was a haven for misfit performers who wanted to practice their art. But now, under David's careful eye and light touch, it was a clear pillar of the community. A shining star. A place to be cherished. A place to be loved.

Lizzie waited at the back of the theater as the crowd cleared. David made eye contact with her a few minutes after the show closed, but he carried on with his crowds of fans and, when he was finished, he waved at the cleaning crew and made his way up to the tech booth without acknowledging her. Lizzie swallowed down the lump in her throat and set her resolve. She let herself out into the lobby, made a quick stop at the bar, and then headed out into the parking lot, finding his car to wait beside it.

CHAPTER 22

Maybe a half hour later, David emerged alone. The lights at the front of the theater had clicked off before his exit, but Lizzie could recognize his shadowy form heading toward the car. He knew it was her, too, and he stopped short. In the darkness, his face began to take shape before her. His heavy brow was knit and, despite the bite in the air, she could see a sheen of sweat at his dark hairline. Without his saying a word, Lizzie could tell that he knew what she'd done at the police station earlier that day. Was her being here too little too late?

She awkwardly held up the drink she had grabbed at the bar.

"Jack and Coke? I had to ask the bartender to make it special since he was closing up."

David's face tensed further, but he reached his hand out and took the drink. He threw his head back and took a swig and then offered it back. "They're not supposed to give out to-go drinks. It's the law."

"Yes, well, turns out a little flirting and saying you know

the owner isn't a bad route to take." She smiled sheepishly. The silence between them hung heavy.

"I was thinking—"

"Do you want—"

They both started to speak at the same time. David laughed at the fumble, sending a wave of relief to wash over Lizzie. He pushed up the sleeves of his blazer, and she noticed once more the climbing, twisting labyrinth of tattoos.

"Listen," she started. "I don't want to ink myself up, so I think I'm just going to have to start stating my regrets out loud if I ever want to put them in the past. I'm sorry I dated Ellis again. That was so freaking stupid. I'm sorry you had to come to my rescue. And I'm sorry you had to come to my rescue again when Fullmer went missing. And when I bailed on the show. But mostly I'm sorry because I never should have left Warner Robins. I never should have disappeared, and not called, and not clung to the one person who always made my world a better place. And I should have told you—" She paused, the words ready and waiting to tumble off her tongue. "I should have told you that Fullmer and Hazel are crazy about you. That they've talked about you every single night since you showed up and baby-sat them when I was gone. That if we left, they'd miss you... that they'd miss their dad."

David looked up at her then. She couldn't read his eyes, so she plowed on, letting the words spill out any way they fell. *You've got this.*

"I didn't think I could tell you. We were only together the one time, and you were going to college and I was going to New York. I was scared that it couldn't work. And then when I couldn't hack it out there, I was ashamed. That little stick showed two lines, and it was like they were crossing out my past here. I couldn't go back. I couldn't do that to you. And I couldn't let anyone know what had happened to me." Lizzie was out of breath. She practically panted, trying to keep up with her own words. "God, I'm sorry, David. I thought about you every day. And if I left again without telling you how I felt, then I would regret it every moment of every day to come. I'm sorry I dragged all of this up with the police. You must feel so—"

He held up a hand to cut her off. Lizzie felt the air refill her lungs, making her dizzy and weak.

"I don't want you to apologize," he said. "I don't want to hear that from you ever again."

She felt a fresh wave of the nausea and rubbed her palms over her eyes as she tried to regain composure. She had hoped he'd respond well. She didn't want—

"What happened to you isn't something that requires an apology." He took a step toward her. She felt the breath catch in her throat. "Going back to Ellis because you were confused and scared isn't something that requires an apology. And going to the police? Exposing what happened with him and being brave enough to face Warner Robins? That's the last thing in the world that requires an apology."

He reached out and took her hands. The skin lit up at his touch, flaming out into a wave of a thousand goosebumps. He looked up at her, eyes open and pleading. "Somehow you are even fiercer than you were back in high school." He laughed a little under his breath. "It's what I always liked about you. And what I missed most while you were away. I... well, Lord. Maybe I have the worst timing in the world, but it's taking all I have not to kiss you right now."

Lizzie felt an explosion of warmth spread from her chest up to her cheeks. He was just as tender and unassuming as he had been back in high school. Unlike all the other men she'd faced, here he was, asking for her permission once again.

"May I—" he started.

This time, she cut him off.

Her kiss nearly knocked him off balance. David pulled her close, his hands gripping the back of her head with a tender strength. Lizzie's knees went weak, and she clutched his arm. The familiar smell of Jack and Coke washed over her, bathing her in warmth and comfort.

Even though she had admitted everything and put it all on the line, the easy intimacy between them had still taken her by surprise. Lizzie had spent close to a decade convincing herself that she was unworthy of being loved, that she was unworthy of being happy. Buying the drink for David and coming to confront him had felt like the beginning of what should be a long, difficult scrap uphill to regain his good graces. The fact that it all came so easy—that he so clearly wanted her and was willing to forget and forgive the past—it was the greatest surprise she'd had in a very long time.

When it was over, he put his forehead to hers and stroked her cheeks with his thumbs. He laughed. This time the sound came easy.

"When I learned about what happened with Ellis, I thought maybe he was—"

"He's not." She confirmed, shaking her head and closing her eyes tight. "He's definitely not."

David cleared his throat. "I hated how much I wanted them to be mine. I didn't dare let myself fully consider the possibility for more than a moment."

"A kid like Fullmer doesn't just inherit that love for jazz out of nowhere," she mused. "God knows I only played bands like The Cranberries when he was a baby."

David laughed again and brought her even closer. "Geez, Lizzie, you got so lucky that those kids grew up to be so cool. I mean, The Cranberries? *Come on.*"

He paused, the real weight of the conversation settling in. His fingers were sending sparks through her skin.

"Look, I don't have any more room on my arms for regret tattoos," he said. "And I'm not going to start in on my face." She kissed him again and hugged him tighter. "So you can't leave again," he admonished. "You're stuck."

Lizzie laughed out loud. All of her nerves from earlier—all the nerves she'd carried with her since the first day she arrived home in Warner Robins—melted away. It was as though no time had passed between them at all. She had picked up right where they left off, the past erased for the better.

A flash in her mind again. But this time, it wasn't a vision of her past. It was the future. She could stay and take care of Nora, take care of her family. She could have friends at the Baron, real friends that weren't nine years old and related to her. Lizzie's children could grow up with a father who listened to Fullmer's jazz music and worried about Hazel flirting with boys.

And she could see herself, happy and loved and finally with a place in Warner Robins to call her own.

"Trust me, I'm not stuck," Lizzie laughed and shook her head. "At this point, I don't think you could get rid of me if you tried."

David slung his arm around her shoulders and pulled her close. "Come back inside with me. We can talk some more."

"I'd like that very much." She smiled.

They began to walk back to the Baron. Lizzie looked up at David in the darkness, admiring the goofy grin he didn't bother to hide. He turned to her quickly as they walked together, suddenly serious. Lizzie felt a rush of embarrassment as she thought he was going to call her out for staring.

"So do you think the kids like me?" He asked, his tone serious and pondering.

"They wouldn't shut up about you from the first time you met them." Lizzie rolled her eyes, joking. She relaxed as the happy, stupid grin returned to David's face once more. He was clearly pleased. "Although I think from the crazy high school stories that you were telling, Hazel is going to think that you'll let her get away with all sorts of shenanigans."

"Oh, no way!" David shook his head. "No boyfriends until she's thirty. At least. And none of those midriff shirts all the girls are wearing. I never understood those..."

Lizzie threw back her head, happy and relaxed. The conversation felt unreal.

Historically, Lizzie Hancock was no good at second chances. But *screw history*, she thought, as she kissed David Flannery again at the front doors of the Baron Theater. This was the blissfully unexpected here and now. Instead of running away this time, maybe she'd run with it.

REVIEW

We hope you've enjoyed From the Top. If you did, please consider leaving a review on Amazon or Goodreads. Reviews can do so much for up and coming authors and your thoughts would be appreciated.

ABOUT THE AUTHOR

Brittni is up and coming in published fiction, but oh-so-familiar to the pen. An accomplished comedian, writer, and performer, she has delighted audiences for years all over the country.

Now she's bringing her wit and attitude to the printed page with heartfelt, sweet, and raw contemporary romance.

Connect on Facebook to hear the latest about her upcoming books!

ALSO BY BRITTNI MINER

Call It Kismet

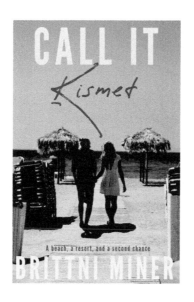

44541247R00115